JIM THOMPSON

SHARECROPPER HELL

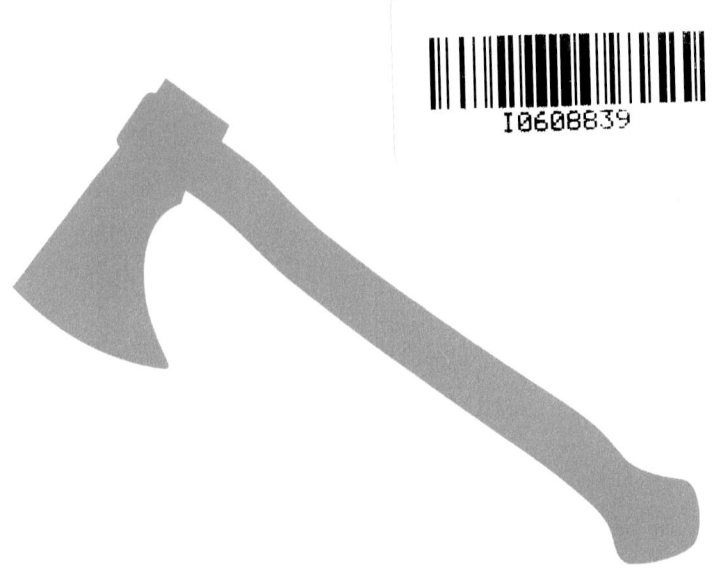

I0608839

CHALK
LINE
BOOKS

ISBN (print edition): 978-1-942531-01-2
ISBN (ebook): 978-0-9896714-1-5
Cover design: Cerný Beran
Title page design: Martina Voríšková
Illustrations: Martha Kelly
Layout design: Patrick Alley

Chalk Line Books is an imprint of
The Devault-Graves Agency, Memphis, Tennessee.
The names Chalk Line Books, Devault-Graves Digital Editions,
and Lasso Books, are all imprints and trademarks of
The Devault-Graves Agency.
www.devault-gravesagency.com

Chapter One

IT WAS ALMOST DUSK, and I knew that meant she'd be waiting for me, her car hidden under the thick willows, waiting just like she had been all along. It was a swell setup.

Her name was Donna. She was one-fourth Indian and three-fourths white, and that's a blood mixture that's hard to beat if you're breeding for beauty. She had the beauty, all right—and plenty more. She could also mean plenty of trouble, if anybody found out about us.

I finished what I was doing and was beginning to feel that don't-give-a-gol-darn crankiness that sneaks up on me when I get real hungry. You know. Maybe you get the same way. You almost hope that someone'll say something to you so you can jump down his throat.

I put the papers in a folder marked

   Miss Trumbull (English Department)
    Burdock County, Oklahoma
    Consolidated School District

and started to slide it into the top drawer of Miss Trumbull's desk. Somehow, one of the papers slipped out and fell into the wastebas-ket; and when I lifted it out I saw this sandwich—part of a sandwich, rather, lying there. It was made out of some kind of fish mixed up with salad dressing and there were little pinkish smears of lipstick on it and a place where spit had hardened. But it smelled awfully good; it looked awfully good. I pinched at it, pinching away the spit and the lipstick. And then, suddenly the classroom door banged open and I shoved the sandwich into my pocket.

It was Abe Toolate, the janitor. I stood up, trying to smile, and he came toward me, his mean little eyes fixed on mine. He stopped right in front of me, so close that I was breathing in the stink of corn liquor, and held out one of his stubby copper-skinned hands.

"I seen you," he grunted. "Let's have it."

"Have what?" I said.

"What you put in your pocket. Been wondering who was doin' all the stealin' around here at night."

I almost laughed in spite of myself. Because he was probably the only person around school that was wondering. Everyone else *knew*; and Abe would have been fired long before if he hadn't had a couple of relatives on the school board.

"Let's have it," he repeated.

"Get away from me," I said. "Get away from me fast, Abe."

"What's your name, boy?" he blustered, as if he didn't know. "What you doing here, anyhow?" And I could feel my face going tight. Shucks, he knew what I was doing there. I'd been grading Miss Trumbull's papers for almost four years, ever since I was a freshman.

I walked straight toward him. I kind of herded him in front of me, backing him toward the cloakroom, and his face began shining with sweat.

"N-now, look, Tom—Tommy," he stuttered. "I didn't mean . . ."

"Tommy?" I said. "Aren't you getting a little familiar, Abe? You mean Mister Carver, don't you?"

"M-mister Carver . . ."

He almost choked on that, having to call a white-trash share-cropper's boy Mister.

I backed him into the cloakroom and stood staring at him a minute or two, watching him sweat and squirm. Then I began to calm down a little, and I wanted to try to patch things up. But I knew there wasn't any way—not after I'd made him put a handle on my name. So I reached down for my football sweater with the big BCS on it, and left.

I walked down the stairs and out the front door thinking about what a funny thing pride was. What a troublesome thing.

Now that my temper had simmered down, I realized that Abe must have seen what I'd stuck in my pocket. He'd tried to dig me in my pride—to give himself a boost by pushing someone else down—and I'd dug right back at him. So, now, or rather tomorrow, there'd be trouble. He'd be in the principal's office the first thing in the morning, and I still wouldn't be able to admit that I'd been going to eat the leavings from Miss Trumbull's lunch.

I dug the sandwich out of my pocket and dropped it down at the side of the steps. Then I slung my sweater around my shoulders and headed across the yard to the road.

It was getting on toward true dark now, but when I rounded the curve that leads down to the creek I saw Donna Ontime's new

Cadillac parked under the willows. Apparently she spotted me at the same time; she gave two short taps on the horn of the car. So I went on, and it sure wasn't hard to do even though I knew what would happen if Pa ever caught us together.

Chapter Two

BEFORE I GO ANY further, perhaps I'd better explain that names like Toolate and Ontime aren't uncommon in Eastern Oklahoma. You see, most of this land over here used to be owned by the Five Civilized Tribes—I mean, the tribes themselves owned it, not individuals in the tribes. That system was all right during territorial days, but before Oklahoma could become a state the land had to be shared out; they had to do away with tribal ownership. So this is the way the government worked it. They set a certain date, right down to the hour, and any child born before that hour got a share of the tribe's property. He got an allotment, as the saying is. But if he was born after that hour—even a minute after it—he didn't get anything. He was just a plain hard-up Indian, unless his kinfolks chose to take care of him.

That's the story behind names like Toolate and Ontime, and a lot of others that have been switched around so much you can hardly recognize 'em for what they were.

Abe Toolate had been born after the allotment hour, and his kin had soon learned better than to heir him anything.

Matthew Ontime, Donna's father, had been born into a good allotment, and he'd inherited from most of his family; and now he owned around five thousand acres. If he'd been willing to lease his land for oilwell drilling, he could have been one of the richest men in Oklahoma. And even without oil he was plenty well-off.

In the back seat of the Cadillac, I looked down into Donna Ontime's smoldering black eyes, and it struck me that I was right on top of, yes, and inside of, more money than you'll find in a pretty big bank. But I'd have liked her just as well if her father hadn't had a penny. I might even have liked her more, if that'd been possible.

She smiled, her teeth white and even in the darkness, and cocked her head a little to one side.

"Well, Tommy?"

"Swell," I said.

"But now you have to go, isn't that right? You have to go, and you think you'd better walk, despite the fact I have to drive right by your place."

"Don't be like that, Donna," I said. "You know I can't help the way Pa feels."

"Never mind, Tommy."

"But what can I do?" I said. "I'm nineteen years old and I'm still in high school, and if I have to drop out for the spring chopping it may take me another year to finish. I have to get along with Pa, at least until I'm out of school."

"Just until, then? No longer, Tommy?"

"Well"—I tried to hedge. "What about your father, Donna? I don't think he's very fond of us Carvers."

"I can handle my father."

"Well, but look! Look, honey," I said. "It's not the same way with me, Donna. I've tried to explain to you that if Pa was really my father—if he hadn't done so much for me—I . . ."

"I understand." She held up a hand, one of the fingers bent down. "Item one: Mr. Carver adopted you back in Mississippi after your own parents were drowned in a flood. Item two: His wife died, and rather than abandon you to an orphanage, he adopted Mary to look after you. I might add that the law seems rather loose when a widower can adopt a fourteen-year-old girl, but. . ."

"I'd rather you didn't say it," I said.

"...but it was probably apparent to the authorities that lust, to Mr. Carver, was just a dirty word in the Bible. Let's see, now, where were we? Oh, yes! Item three: the doctors thought you belonged in a higher, dryer climate, so Mr. Carver left Mississippi and brought you and Mary here. . . . That's quite a lot for a man to do, isn't it? All for the sake of helping an infant, who wasn't even related to him, to become a man."

"I think it's quite a bit, yes," I said.

"I haven't overlooked anything?"

I shrugged. "I guess not."

"But *you've* overlooked something. You were out in the fields doing a man's work when you were six years old, and you've never known anything but work since then. All you've got out of life is enough food to keep you working and enough beatings to kill two mules."

"I've got more than that," I said. "And Pa isn't really mean. He's just kind of old-fashioned and strict."

"I see. Well, that makes everything all right, then."

"No," I said, "you don't see, Donna. But I guess I won't be able to talk any more about it now. I would like to have you drive me home, though, if . . ."

"I know. If it wasn't for Pa."

"That wasn't what I was going to say. I was going to say that I could scoot down in the seat and you could drive on past our place and . . ."

She got up abruptly, not speaking, and slid over into the front seat. She started the motor with a roar, slammed in the gears, and sent the car leaping out of the willows and onto the road. I climbed over into the front seat and scooted down, holding on for dear life. The car was doing eighty by this time, sailing and bouncing over the red-clay ruts. But there wasn't a thing I could do. She was all-out Indian-mad; and when they get that way, you can't reason with 'em.

I'd seen her this way just once before; spring a year ago it was, right after she'd finished at the state university. She had a big Chrysler then, and she'd got a flat two-three miles out of the village; and I offered to fix it for her. I knew her, of course, since we share-crop forty acres for Matthew Ontime in addition to our own ten. But it was only in a nodding, good-morning-miss way.

Well, I went to work on the tire, and I don't know as I said anything—rather, it was what I didn't say. The way I acted, sort of too-casual, and indifferent. Because when you've been raised by a man like Pa, you're bound to absorb some of his ideas even when you know they're completely unreasonable. Pa was always telling about how the Five Tribes had been forced out of Georgia and Mississippi and Florida, back in the early 1800's; and how they should have been crowded right on out into the Pacific Ocean, instead of being allowed to hog onto good land that the white folks needed. He was always saying that they were all streaked with the tar-brush—that they were part nigger. He claimed they were lazy and thieving, loaded with all kinds of dirty diseases. And I'd soon learned better than to argue with him. I'd had to listen and listen, never saying anything back, until his way of thinking had almost become mine.

So, I guess I was pretty off-hand with Donna; insulting without saying or doing anything. Anyway, she took it up to a point, not seeming to notice. And then—and I don't know how else to put it—she just went crazy. I was hunkered down, sliding the hub-cap into place, when it happened. I heard a moan, the kind you might hear from a hurt-crazy bobcat. Then she had thrown herself at me, knocking me backwards to the road; and she went down on top of me, kicking and pounding and scratching and biting. And I realized, vaguely, that she was actually trying to kill me. But what I was thinking mostly was that even with her black hair tangled and her face smeared with the dirt of the road, she must be the prettiest girl in the world. I was thinking about what she'd be like, what she was bound to be like, under her clothes.

It stopped as suddenly as it had started. There wasn't any lead-up to it. It was just gone, like a grass fire hit by a flash flood. She went completely motionless, looking at me wide-eyed like she couldn't believe what had happened. Then she buried her head against my chest and began to cry. I picked her up and set her in the car, and . . .

Well, that's the way it started. That's the way she was. I hope she snapped out of this mad before she wrapped us around a cottonwood.

We went up a rise in the road, I could feel the car shoot upward. Then the brakes went on so hard that I almost slid under the dashboard, and we swung to the left, horn blaring, clear into the ditch. And there was a blinding flash of light and someone yelled, and another horn blared—and I knew we'd almost run down another car. Then, we were back on the road again, still traveling fast but a lot slower than we had been; and Donna laughed softly.

She reached over and pulled my head down into her lap. She scooted forward a little, and I knew she wanted me to put my arms around her hips, so I did. We rode on in silence until we made the turn into Ontime plantation, which was also the turn into our place.

"Perhaps it's best this way," she said, thoughtfully, as if she'd been arguing with herself. "I know I wouldn't like it if you were like the others—kow-towing and falling all over your feet because of the money."

She'd told me about that, how she'd felt about the university crowd; and I liked her enough—so much—that I'd tried to talk her out of it. I wanted her to have the breaks that she deserved; so I told her again that she might be a little hard on people.

"Perhaps," she said. "But you can't help thinking those things.

And it's such a wonderful feeling when you know there's someone who's not influenced the least by money, even if . . ."

"Yes," I said.

"I'm like Dad, I guess. I'd rather see someone with the wrong principles than no principles at all."

"Donna, you know . . ."

"I know." She lowered a hand from the wheel and stroked my head. "By the way, I think that was your father we passed back there."

"I thought I recognized his voice," I said. "Could you tell who he was with?"

"I'm afraid—well, it was a red and white car, darling, so I ..."

"Oh, my gosh," I said, and I sat up.

A red and white car—it was bound to be one of the oil-company scouts. I'd thought they all knew, by now, that they were wasting their time in trying to lease our ten acres because Matthew Ontime wouldn't lease his, and we were almost spang in the middle of his land. All of 'em should have known it. But, now, here was another one, a new man probably, and he'd be a fast talker like all the lease-hounds were. He'd dangle a fortune in front of Pa, and Pa would ache for it, mainly for what it would mean to me, and he wouldn't be able to touch it.

At the best, he'd be deep-down bitter for days, twice as hard to live with as he usually was. At the worst . . .? Well, it would be bad enough if he only tried to *talk* to Donna's father. If he only did *that*.

"I wish I could help, darling. Dad will listen to me about a lot of things, but . . ."

"You mustn't try to talk to him," I said. "He'd wonder why you were interested, and—well, anyway, I think he's right. He doesn't need money. There's no reason why he should lease just to accommodate Pa."

"I would." She hesitated. "If I could persuade Dad to give me my inheritance now . . ."

"Let's not talk about it," I said.

"No," she nodded, slowly, "perhaps we'd better not. Shall I drive on past your house, Tommy?"

"No need," I said. "Mary won't say anything."

She throttled the Cadillac down, glancing up into the rearview mirror to make sure that the oil-company car was still out of sight.

"Mary knows about us, doesn't she, Tommy?"

"Well . . . she knows I'm with you whenever I can be. I've had to have her cover up for me a time or two, and . . ."

"She hates me, Tommy."

"Why, that's crazy!" I laughed. "She feels like she has to go along with Pa on everything, sure. You might say she hasn't got a real will of her own, and probably she acts like . . ."

"It wasn't acting. I've seen her in town a few times, with your father, and she's looked at me and . . ." Her voice trailed off.

"You're imagining things," I said, and I opened the door of the car.

"Tommy. How old is she?"

"Around thirty-three, I guess. She was somewhere around fourteen or fifteen when Pa took her in."

"She's never gone with anyone? Any men?"

"No. Maybe she's been too afraid of Pa, but I kind of think she's never been interested."

"Strange, isn't it? And she's—she could be quite attractive."

"She looks all right, I guess," I said shortly, because somehow I was getting uncomfortable. "I'll have to go now, Donna."

"But," she looked up into the mirror. "Yes, I guess you'd better. Try to keep him from coming over to our house, darling. I'm always afraid he—that he and Dad might—And it would change us, Tommy! We wouldn't want it to, but . . ."

"I'll try. God knows I'll do my best," I said.

She kissed me quickly and then drove away. I ran crouching across the road to the house.

It was, well, I don't know how many times it was that I'd seen her. But now that she was gone, it seemed as incredible as it had the first time. It was hard to believe that it had happened. She had everything, she was everything a man could want.

I glanced back over my shoulder and made a spurt toward the porch.

The chances were that I'd be a mighty sore-backed ploughhand if I wasn't a little more careful.

Chapter Three

MOST PEOPLE THINK OF Oklahoma as being new country, a place that wasn't settled until the last forty years or so, and that's reasonably true of part of it. But it doesn't hold for the south and southeast section.

The Five Civilized Tribes—the Creeks, Choctaws, Chickasaws, Cherokees and Seminoles—started moving in around 1817. They came up from the deep south, blazing the Trail of Tears as they called it; and they established five Indian nations with towns and courts and schools and newspapers, and, well, about everything you'd find in any country of the period. Because maybe they had reason to hate the white people, but they'd lived too long like whites to change. They farmed like whites, they and the slaves they brought with them; they cottoned and corned the land to death. It began losing topsoil, then subsoil; and by the time of statehood there were whole counties that weren't producing a fourth of what they should have.

The state and federal governments finally woke up and tried to build the soil back up. But the share-crop system just naturally doesn't attract people with much brains; if they understood anything about scientific farming and all, they wouldn't be croppers in the first place. Anyway, it's hard to show a man where he can gain by improving land he doesn't own.

So, as late as fifteen years ago, when we moved in from Mississippi, a lot of land was still going to pot—and it still is—and probably it's a good thing it was. Otherwise we'd never even have been able to buy ten acres from one of Matthew Ontime's kin.

We'd never got any more than that because that was another farm that Matthew fell heir to, and he knew what could be done with worn-out land as well as Pa. He knew a lot more about the subject than Pa did.

So all we had and were ever going to have was those ten acres, and the two tenant shacks and outbuildings that had come with 'em. But that was something; it was a big step up from being ordinary croppers, and we'd made the most of it.

We'd placed the two shacks end-to-end, with a screened-in breezeway connecting them, and we'd torn down one of the outbuildings and built a long porch across the front. We'd rubbed down the floors with sandstone and varnished 'em—they're probably the only cropper-house floors in the country with varnish. And we'd painted the outside white with a green trim; and that's something else you don't see often—a painted house—in cropper country. It looked real nice, for what it was.

I reached the porch just as the oil scout's car slowed down for the turn into the yard.

Mary snatched the sweater out of my hands. She thrust a bucket at me with a little water in it and disappeared inside the house. I hadn't needed to tell her a thing. She'd known just what to do.

I poured the water into the wash basin and jerked up my sleeves. By the time the car lights hit me, I was bent over the washbench, busy as all getout.

I'd just brought in an armload of firewood, maybe, and now I was scrubbing up for dinner.

The car stopped in the yard, and for a minute or so there was a heavy silence. Then the lease scout—I couldn't see what he looked like—cleared his throat. And I picked up the water bucket and sauntered down toward the well.

"I just can't understand," he said, irritated and trying to sound like he wasn't. "I've been in this business all my life, Mr. Carver, and I can't . . ."

"I'm trying to tell you, mister . . ."

"Is there anything that isn't clear to you? What more could you ask for? We'll give you a royalty of one-eighth of the production, the usual production royalty; no one can give you more than that. But we'll pay you an advance against that royalty of twenty-five hundred dollars an acre . . ."

Twenty-five hundred! That was two-fifty more an acre than the last offer we'd had.

". . . think of it, Mr. Carver! We pay you twenty-five thousand dollars—tuh-wenty-fi-uhv thousand—cash on the barrelhead! And that's just a starter. Why, if this area here is even half as rich as our geologists' report, you'll . . ."

Pa groaned. He actually groaned, and without seeing him I knew the way his face was twisting like a man in agony.

". . . tuh-wenty-fi-uv thousand dol—"

"Stop it! Durn your hide, stop it! Don't you say another word!"

"But I don't under . . ."

"I've been tryin' to tell you!" Pa yelled. "I've been tryin' to tell you for an hour, now! You can't lease my ten acres! You *can't*! Your company wouldn't let you!"

The scout started to butt in again, but Pa yelled him down. "Don't you reckon I know? I've seen it tried, man! They'd have to check over the lease before the money was paid, and they'd find out that my little ten here was all they could get! And they wouldn't touch it then with a ten-foot pole! They couldn't hope to more'n break even, if they were lucky enough to do that!"

"If you'd just leave that to . . ."

"I ain't going to leave it to you! I ain't gonna let you waste your time or mine. What's it cost to drill a deep well, anyway? A hundred to a hundred and fifty thousand dollars, right? So you can't just have you enough room for one well; an' you put two or three down side by side you don't gain nothing. They just drain each other off. Before you could drill on my acreage, you'd want everything in sight under lease! And that biggety Indian won't let you have one single acre! Not one, mister."

The scout laughed. A match flared as he lighted a cigarette. "Well, now, I'm sure if we offered him the right kind of proposition . . ."

"All right, mister," said Pa, wearily. "All right."

"It's a deal, then? You and I have a deal?"

"You go talk to him," said Pa. "Or go talk to some of the oilmen around town. Then come back and see me."

"Agreed! We'll call it a deal, Mr. Carver. I'll bring an attorney out tomorrow morning, and . . ."

"No," said Pa. "You won't be coming back, tomorrow morning or any other time. But I ain't goin' to argue with you about it."

He got out of the car, swinging the white meal sack full of groceries over his shoulders. He stood back to let the scout drive off, and then he went plodding up toward the house, not looking at me; probably not even seeing me. I emptied the water bailer into my bucket and ran and caught up with him.

"Here, Pa," I said, "let me take that."

"Huh?" he blinked at me. "Oh. Howdy, boy. How's school?"

"Fine," I said.

"You're showin' 'em, huh? You ain't slackin' up any? You're showin' 'em what us Carvers can do?"

"Yes, sir," I said.

I eased the meal sack onto my shoulder, but he still stood blinking at me, looking at me and through me. He was as tall as I was, tall and wiry. But years of cropping had pushed his chest in, curving his back and neck, and he had to bend his head back to look at me. His leathery upturned face made me think of one of those big snapping turtles that grab hold of something and never let go.

"You see that fool Indian girl?" he said.

"Indian girl?"

"Almost ran me and that oil feller into the ditch. Good thing she ain't my daughter. I'd peel the hide right off of her."

"Yes, sir," I said.

He went on into the house, nodded absently at Mary and entered his bedroom—the bedroom and the kitchen were the only two rooms in that house, the one on the south end of the breezeway. My room and Mary's and what passed as a sitting room was in the other house.

He'd closed the door but we didn't have real walls between our rooms, just two by eleven plank partitions, and I heard him sigh and drop down on his cornshuck mattress. I gave Mary a grin, letting her know that everything was all right, and we began unloading the groceries.

"Hungry, Tom?" she said softly.

"That's not the word for it," I said.

"You want a sweet potato while you're waitin'? I got them and the greens done."

"I guess I can hold out until supper," I said.

I unwrapped the slab of side meat and started slicing it into strips. She ripped open the sack of flour, began measuring double handfuls into a crockery bowl.

"Him," she muttered, "just too mean to live, that's what he is."

"Aw, now, Mary," I grinned, "You don't really mean that."

"I do so!" She tossed salt and baking powder into the flour. "Hardly a bite in this house since yesterday morning, all on account o' his meanness! He was in town yesterday, wasn't he? Why couldn't he've bought groceries then instead of today?"

"Well," I said, "you know how Pa figures. We've only got so much to spend for food. If we eat it all up at one time . . ."

"*Who* eats it all? Who eats more around here than anyone else?"

I shrugged. "Well, he has to do without, too."

"Yeah," she said, bitterly. "I just bet he does! He wants him a sandwich or a sody pop or somethin', he buys it. I see *him* doin' without anything!"

I told her she'd better keep her voice down, and she turned a little pale, glancing at the partition. Then, since there wasn't much else I could help with, I crossed over through the breezeway to the parlor.

It was the best fixed-up room in the place, and it was a pretty good best, considering. Mary had made the big hooked rug. She'd made the dyed flour-sack curtains. She'd woven the raffia mattings that padded the two easy chairs and the little settee. Pa and I had made the bases of the furniture—rustic, you'd call it—but the bent-willow arms and backs, the parts that really prettied it up, were Mary's work. Excepting the little packing-box center table, and, of course, the kerosene lamp and the big old-time Bible, practically everything in the room had been made by Mary.

I lighted the lamp, turning the flame down low to keep the wick from smoking. I looked around me, at the rug, the furniture and curtains; and, suddenly, for no reason I could think of, I blew the lamp out again. I stood there in the semi-darkness, the first rays of moonlight seeping through the windows, and I looked out of the room because I no longer liked it—I liked it but it made me uncomfortable—I stared across the breezeway and into the kitchen.

How old . . . ?

Quite attractive . . . ?

She plodded back and forth from the stove to the table, from table to cupboard. Her bare brown legs rose tapering and strong from the old unlaced ploughshoes, an old pair of mine. The faded gingham dress clung to her body, swelling and filling and curving, as she reached up to the cupboard or bent over the table. Her breasts, her pear-shaped hips, her belly, her . . .

I sat down, trembling a little. I took out my bandanna and wiped the sweat from my face, wiped my hands.

I didn't need to imagine. I knew what they—what all of her was like. And why shouldn't I? I thought. Why shouldn't I know and remember? She'd been like a mother to me. She'd been almost the same as the mother I'd never known.

No, there hadn't been anything wrong back then, back when I was a tot. There was nothing wrong in knowing and remembering; and there was nothing wrong now. It was right to kiss her goodnight; it was right to hug her and pat her when she was feeling blue and lonesome and beaten down.

It was right. It was just as it should be. Everything was the same as it always had been except that I'd let Donna put a crazy notion in my head. That was the whole trouble, and I'd better get over it fast. Because I had some real troubles to worry about.

I'd have a mess to face at school tomorrow. And, probably, if Pa did what I thought he would, there'd be an even worse fracas tonight with Matthew Ontime.

Mary called out that supper was ready.

We all sat down at the oilcloth-covered kitchen table, and Pa said a bless-this-bounty-Lord, and we ate.

I'd been half-starved fifteen minutes before. But sometimes, you know, when you get too hungry, you lose your appetite; and I guess that was the trouble with me. Mary kept passing me dishes, and I'd pass 'em back. I'd take a little sometimes, but more often I wouldn't. I just couldn't eat much.

"You sick?" she said, finally.

"Oh, no," I said. "Just not very hungry."

"You ought to be hungry. What's the matter?"

"What's the matter with *you*?" said Pa, looking up from his plate. "Why'n't you stop gabbing all the time?"

"Y-yes, sir," said Mary.

"He knows whether he's hungry or not. He ain't no baby."

"Yes, sir," said Mary again.

It was funny to watch her. Kind of sad-funny. The minute his back was turned she couldn't say enough against him or do enough; although there wasn't really anything that she could do. But she couldn't face up to him for as much as a second. When he spoke to her or looked at her, she went down like a sunflower under a hoe. That was one side of Pa, the way he treated Mary, that was awfully hard to take.

Pa pushed back his plate and poured coffee into his saucer. He lifted it up, letting his eyes stray off to the right. And my heart skipped a beat. I knew what he was considering as he stared at the long shelf where the double-barreled shotgun lay.

He squinted thoughtfully. Then, he sighed and gave his head a little shake. He put the saucer down on the oilcloth. His mouth twitched.

"God damn him," he said, and he was praying not cursing. "God damn his black soul to hell!"

He glared from me to Mary, his leathery face working; and he raised his hand and slapped it against the table.

"I'm gonna *make* him! I'm gonna make him, you hear me?"

"All right, Pa," I said. I knew there wasn't any use arguing with him.

"Come on! We'll go right now."

I pushed my chair back and got up. All I could hope for was that he would not say anything to Matthew Ontime about Donna. Matthew had taken a lot off of Pa—more than he had any call to—but I knew there'd be fireworks if Pa said anything about his only daughter. Donna was the only family he had, his wife being dead, and Indians set a heap of store by their families.

"Pa"—I hesitated—"there's just one thing . . ."

"Yes," said Mary, her voice strangely loud. "Don't forget to tell him off about that crazy girl of his!"

It was probably the only time in her life she'd ever spoken up to Pa, and you can imagine how he took it. Up until then, I'm pretty sure, he had intended to speak his mind about Donna. But wild horses couldn't have made him do it now. He couldn't do something that she told him to do.

If I hadn't been a little sore at Mary, I'd have felt sorry for her.

"Now, that'd make a lot of sense, wouldn't it?" he jeered, his head thrust forward on his neck like a turkey gobbler's.

Mary didn't say anything. She'd started to fold up as soon as the words were out of her mouth.

"Supposin' something happened to him, and I had to deal with her," he said, arguing with himself, convincing himself. "How you reckon she'd act after I'd low-downed her to her Daddy? Hey? You think I'd want her feelin' mean and stubborn toward me?"

It was a good argument. I hoped he remembered it. "You're dead right, Pa," I said. "You're a thousand percent right."

"'Course I am," he nodded. "Anyone but that danged id-jit could see it. Why, for all we know ol' Ontime might be dead right now. He mightn't even live the week out. An' what would a flighty girl want with runnin' a plantation?"

"Yes, sir," I said.

"Why, any number o' things could happen to him," he went on. "Someone might decide to take that uppitiness out of him, or he might tumble off one of them pranky horses, or . . ." He broke off, glaring at Mary as though she'd disputed him. "You tellin' me it couldn't happen? You think I don't know what I'm talkin' about?"

"N-no, s-sir."

"Better not, either." He jutted his chin out. "Grab your sweater, Tom."

"Yes, sir," I said.

Chapter Four

I'M NINETEEN, NOT A man yet according to the law. But I've got to go a long way back to remember when I wasn't one otherwise. A man in thinking, acting, working.

You grow up fast in cotton country, or you don't grow up. You stop being a child just about as soon as you're out of the cradle. You're concerned with cornbread not cookies, beds not bedtime stories. You're part of something that always has a little heavier load than it can carry, that always has to put out more than it can get back. So you hold up your end, or it falls on you. You don't drag your feet, or you get left behind.

We walked along silently, one of us on each side of the road where the walking was easiest, the brown-dry Bermuda grass rustling against our shoes. The first frost was in the air. Out in the fields the dead cotton plants drooped sleepily.

It didn't seem loyal to Pa to wish for the time when I'd be my own man. Because that was like wishing he was dead; he'd want me until then. So I didn't wish—not more'n a little when I thought about Donna; no more than I could keep from wishing—but I couldn't help thinking.

Pa wouldn't be able to turn his lease. But it wouldn't really change anything if he did. We'd eat better, dress better; I'd get to go to college. But there wouldn't be any real change. I'd still be Pa's man, doing what he liked, doing nothing that he didn't like.

I owed it to him.

I was so wrapped up in my thinking that I didn't hear him for a few seconds after he spoke. It took that long for the words to register.

"What?" I said. "Why, no, I wanted to come with you, Pa."

"You really did?"

"Sure, I did. Naturally."

"Well," he said, doubtfully. "Maybe I shouldn't've let you, though. I don't want nothin' but good for you, son. You're gonna be someone, and I can't let no trouble fall in your way."

"I'll be all right," I said.

"Me, I don't matter. The Lord put his curse on me long ago, and there ain't nothin' left but atonement. I lost my license to live. The Lord Jehovah took it away in His righteous wrath, an' I could no longer dwell in His image, and He gave me penance . . ."

He went on talking, mumbling, with me putting in a "Yes, sir," now and then, but not really listening. I'd heard the same talk, with variations, a thousand times before, from him and at the backwoods revival meetings I was dragged to. I never could cipher out how people with so much work to do and so little money could do so much sinning. But they all seemed to do a lot.

We came to the long grove of cottonwoods that led up to the plantation. We came out of it and paused, staring at the big white house with its columned portico; and I heard Pa swallow hard. We went on, our feet dragging a little, and the road began to branch off into graveled, cedar-lined drives, and Pa stopped again.

He looked at me, waiting, and I knew what he wanted me to say.

"Think we ought to go around to the back, Pa?"

"What for? Why'n't we march right up to the front?"

"Well, it's closer around to the back," I lied. "I don't see why we should put ourselves out any for him."

"Yeah. Well . . ."

"Anyway, he'll be making a late patrol before he turns in. We may be able to catch him out at the stables."

He gave in, like he'd intended to in the first place. We followed the drive around to the rear, and headed across the back lawn to the outbuildings. There was a passel of them, all painted white, spread out along neat drives and walks like a little city. Dairy barn, hog sheds, chicken houses, smoke house, implement sheds, blacksmith shop, stables . . .

I hadn't actually believed we'd find him there. I'd meant to rouse up one of the hands and send him to the house with a message. But there he came, Matthew Ontime, I mean. We were a few paces short of the stable door when he came through it, leading one of his big bay riding horses.

He saw us and stopped. Then he dropped the reins of the horse and came toward us.

He was probably as old as Pa, but he looked twenty years younger. His shoulders seemed a yard broad under his suede jacket. His head was bared, and the thick barbered hair was as black as Donna's. And his teeth were as white and even. He spoke pleasantly, in a voice that was something like hers, slapping the riding crop against his corduroy trousers.

"Mr. Carver," he nodded to us. "Tom."

It was a big courtesy, his calling Pa mister, but he might not have meant it as such. Knowing what he did about Pa, he may have done it for his own sake. A man like him had to be mistered, and this was the only way he could swing it.

"Is this a social visit"—there was the faintest edge to the words— "or business? I don't want to hurry you, but I was just . . ."

"It's about the oil," said Pa.

"Oil? Coal oil, you mean? You need some kerosene for the house?"

"No, that ain't what I mean," said Pa. He knew he'd started off wrong, sounded foolish, and it got his dander up. "I'm talking about the oil under my land that I can't get out account of you."

"I see. Perhaps I'm in error, but I thought I'd explained my position on that matter."

"I had another offer today. Twenty-five hundred an acre. Twenty-five thousand in cash, against an eighth royalty."

"And?"

"And," said Pa. "That's all you can say, *and*? I ain't fitten for field work much longer and I ain't got no way of helpin' Tom—help him to be somethin' aside what I been—I ain't got nothin' and I can't never get nothin' except this way. An' you stand there an' say *and!*"

Matthew Ontime had stopped swinging the riding crop. For the first time he sounded really friendly instead of put-on friendly. "Believe me, Mr. Carver," he said, "I can understand your feelings and sympathize with them. But I think there must be some solution to your problems, other than turning a five-thousand-acre plantation, with sixty families on it, into an oil field. Tom's an excellent scholar"—he smiled at me—"Yes, I know your reputation, Tom . . ."

"Thank you," I said.

"I'm sure he could get a scholarship and a student loan, and . . ."

"An' how about the farm? How'd I keep it goin' without him to help?"

"You're cropping forty for me now? Cut it down to twenty and I'll increase your share enough to make up for the cut."

"We don't want no gifts," said Pa. "All we want is what we're entitled to."

"Well, I'm afraid . . ." Matthew hesitated. "What did you pay for your ten, Mr. Carver? Fifty—fifty-five an acre?"

"Fifty. But . . ."

"I know. You've put in a great many improvements, done wonders with it. So suppose I do this, since you're dissatisfied and need ready cash. You can go on cropping shares with me, as much or as little land as you like, and I'll take the ten off your hands. I'll give you a hundred and a quarter—no, I'll make that a hundred and fifty an acre."

"A hundred and fifty!" Pa yelled it out.

"Yes. That seems fair, don't you think so, Tom?"

It was much more than fair. But even if I'd been of a mind to say so, I didn't get the chance.

"Fair!" Pa yelled. "I just got through tellin' you I was offered twenty-five hundred a acre!"

"But that was for the mineral rights." Matthew spoke carefully, like he was talking to a child. "It's not worth that as farm land."

"'Course it ain't! Why else'd I be wantin' to lease it for oil?"

"But . . ." Matthew laughed shortly, irritably. A lot less irritably, I reckon, than he felt. Reaching behind him he grasped the reins of his horse. "Don't you think, Mr. Carver," he said, "you're being just a little unreasonable?"

"What's unreasonable about wantin' twenty-five thousand dollars? I got a right to it, ain't I? It's my land, ain't it?"

"And the five thousand adjoining acres are mine. Surely, you can't expect me to . . ."

"Naw, I don't expect you to! Don't expect you to do nothin' that's decent an' makes sense! You don't need money. You got yours, an' you don't care if anybody else has nothin' or not!"

"Now, Mr. Carver . . ."

"To heck with you!"

"Please. You've come here to get this matter straightened out. Now, let's get it straight . . ."

I was getting pretty puzzled; puzzled along with the uneasiness. Because Matthew Ontime didn't have to take lip from anyone, let alone a sharecropper, and he'd never been known to do it. Until now.

I almost shook my head, wondering, watching the straight, proud way he stood, watching the flash of his black eyes, the white even teeth. And the reason came to me—the only reason he could have for doing it. And I felt awfully happy, but also sad. And scared.

I remember how Donna had been the day I'd stopped to fix her tire. Cool and pleasant one second, a devil out of hell the next.

"... the only thing that's real, Mr. Carver. You know how much just a little land can mean to a man. Growing land. Land held in fee simple. You can take care of it, and it takes care of you. Now, it's true that I have far more than the average share, but—well, that's the point, in a way, don't you see? Why should I sacrifice a way of life, and the principles I live by, to get more? Now . . ."

"Yeah, but I ain't . . ."

"Let me finish, please. Let's examine every side of this question. It takes years before land that's been drilled for oil can be brought back to farm land. Sometimes it can never be brought back. It's worthless, eroded and gullied, soaked with oil and salt water. And what happens to the people who farm that land? What would happen to the sixty families who work this plantation?"

Pa grunted. "What do I care what happens to 'em? A bunch o' white trash an' niggers and half-breeds!"

"I see," said Matthew Ontime, slowly. "Is that your attitude also, Tom?"

"You're talkin' to *me*," snapped Pa.

"I'm speaking to Tom. What about it, Tom?"

I waited. Pa jerked his head. "Go ahead, boy. Answer him."

"Yes, sir," I said. I forced the words out. "That's my attitude."

"I'm sorry. But perhaps it's just as well. Now, you'll have to excuse me."

He started to turn toward his horse. Pa leaped forward and

caught him by the arm. "I ain't through talkin' to you, you . . . !"

I couldn't see what happened, it was so fast. But Pa suddenly rose up in the air, and when he came down again he was a good two yards from where he'd been standing. He landed on his feet, upright, but it took all of the breath out of him.

"It would seem," said Matthew Ontime, quietly, "that I'm not through talking to you either. You're not cropping for me any longer, Carver. I'm dividing your forty among my other tenants."

"B-but what'll I . . ."

"I don't give a damn, Carver. But if I find you on my land after tonight, you'll be treated as a common trespasser."

He nodded curtly and put a hand on the saddle pommel. And Pa was screaming, "You dirty half-breed! You . . . !" And Matthew was on the horse, and the horse was wheeling, rearing, its hooves raised high in the air. And Pa stumbled backwards and fell, rolled screaming but no longer cursing. And the hooves came down, barely missing him, and raised high again.

I came to my senses and sprang.

I took a running spring, arms spread. And Matthew Ontime came out of the saddle with me on top of him. I clubbed my fist and hit him once, twice. Then I staggered up, back, looking down at him, at her, watching him as he sat up, brushing blood from his face.

"What you bawlin' for? What's the matter, you idjit?"

Pa was shaking me by the arm. Pulling me toward the road. "Come on, dang you! We hang around here an' . . ."

The barnyard floodlights were coming on, and doors were slamming, and heavy feet were pounding toward us.

We ran.

Chapter Five

IT RAINED DURING THE night and it was still misty in the morning. But Pa was off for town the minute he'd gulped his breakfast. He knew that Matthew Ontime would have too much pride to put the law on us for what had happened, so he couldn't get into town fast enough. He could go around crowing about how *we'd* beaten up one of the richest men in Oklahoma, and he'd be perfectly safe.

I set off for school earlier than I usually did, almost looking forward to the trouble I'd find there. You know—or maybe you don't. Maybe you don't know how it is when you're so sick inside, sick and hopeless-feeling, that you want someone to cross you a little; just enough so's you'll have an excuse to make them feel bad, too.

Ordinarily, at least in the winter when the land was fallowing, I cut across fields to the county road. But this morning I had to go around by the plantation road, the one Donna'd brought me home on. There wasn't any doubt in my mind that Matthew Ontime'd meant just what he said about trespassing. As far as that plantation went, he was the law; in fact, both of his overseers had deputy sheriff commissions. They wouldn't haul you into court unless they caught you stealing or some such thing. But they were apt to make you wish that they would take you to court.

I walked along in the mist, my sweater dampening.

Down near the intersection of the county, Nate Laverty whistled at me; and he and his brother Pete came running down the path from their shack. They were big, thin, bucktoothed kids, about my age but several grades behind me. Pete asked me why'n hell I was all bundled up in a sweater. I didn't see him and Nate wearing sweaters, did I? What kind of a sissy was I? he laughed.

"You haven't got a sweater," I said. "You haven't got anything but those ragged-assed overalls and your mealbag shirts."

Nate's face fell. Pete tried to spit, easy like, like he hadn't heard me; and his teeth got in the way, spilling it over his chin.

"Shucks," I laughed. "Don't you know when a man's kidding? Why, if I hadn't made the football team I'd have been worse off'n you guys."

"What you mean, worse off'n *us*," said Pete. "We're doin' all right."

"Goddammit!" I yelled; and they stopped, startled. They knew I'd never cursed before. "Goddammit"—it was easy now—"stop picking me up on everything!"

"Hey," said Pete, "someone been steppin' on your tail, boy?"

"I—Pa and I had a run-in with Matthew Ontime. He's takin' our acreage away from us."

"Yeah?" Their eyes got wide. "How come?"

"Because he's a no-good son-of-a-bitch, that's why!"

"Mr. Ontime? You must be talkin' about someone else, fella."

"Goddammit, I'm talkin' about . . ."

"Yes, sir," said Pete, firmly, "you sure must be talkin' about some-one else. There never was a fairer man than Mr. Ontime *nowheres!*"

The school doors were open, because of the drizzle, and we went on in. They left me on the first landing, since their homerooms were on that floor. I went up the stairs to the second. And there was Miss Trumbull, waiting for me.

She smiled and spoke, her pince-nez glasses sparkling so's you couldn't see her eyes. She was a prim, pretty strict old lady, and a lot of the students didn't like her. But she'd always been awfully nice to me.

"Will you step into Mr. Redbird's office with me, Thomas? I told him we'd be in as soon as you arrived."

"What for?" I said. "I haven't done anything."

"Certainly you haven't. Mr. Redbird knows it and I know it."

"Well, then . . ."

"Come along, Thomas." She took me by the arm, and I went along.

We went into the principal's office, and she closed the door. He smiled at her and winked at me, and we sat down on the other side of his desk.

He was dark, of course; dark-haired and dark-eyed. He taught my science class, along with being principal, and we'd always got along real well.

"Well, Tom," he grinned, "we have a terrible accusation against you. Our esteemed custodian, Mr. Toolate, tells us . . ."

"I know what he told you. Why'n't you have him here to tell me?"

"Well, now . . ."

"That awful man!" Miss Trumbull clucked her tongue. "I really can't blame Thomas for being annoyed."

"He's not worth getting annoyed," Mr. Redbird shrugged. "We have to put up with him, it seems, but—Tom, just what was the trouble? There's been some light-fingered work around here in . . ."

"Yes, and you know who's behind it!"

"I've got a pretty good idea, yes. Tell us what happened. Were you teasing Abe—trying to get a rise out of him?"

"He tried to get smart with me," I said, "and I threw a scare into the dirty half-breed!"

"Thomas!" said Miss Trumbull. And her face went all tight and funny.

But Mr. Redbird kept on smiling. "Tell me you didn't put anything in your pocket, Tom," he said. "That's all you need to do."

"I suppose you'd take my word against his!"

"Of course I would."

I hesitated. But I was so sick inside, and what was the use anyway. "Sure you would! You'd side against one of your own kind! Why do you try to cover it up, anyway? Why'n't you spell your name right—Red Bird—instead of pushin' yourself off as a white man? Why . . ."

"Get out," he said, "get out, get out, g-ggg . . ."

Miss Trumbull jumped up in front of me. She jerked me up and whirled me around and shoved me out the door, and she sure moved fast and strong for a little old lady.

"Get your books, Thomas! You're on indefinite suspension."

"Shove the books," I said. "I'm not coming back."

And I ran down the stairs and out of the building. I heard her faintly, calling after me, *Thomas! Thomas Carver!* Then the bell for the first class started ringing; and I couldn't hear anything else. The sound followed me down the road, and I had to bang my ears with my palms to drive it away.

I came to the draw under the willows where Donna usually parked. I walked back in under the trees and hunkered down against a rock, thinking if I sat there awhile, maybe until noon, she'd show up. Because she had done that several times. She'd drive by the school, just before twelve, signaling with the horn. And I'd run down at noon, and we'd have as much as a half-hour together. But—but I didn't reckon she'd be here today.

Not today or any other day.

I walked on toward home, and the mist turned into a hard, chilling rain. I was soaked in no time, and I hardly seemed to notice. It just didn't matter.

Donna. Donna . . .

"Huh-uh, boy. Never again."

"But I could! I could slip up there at night . . ."

"Yeah. And maybe get your tail shot off!"

"I got to try! She'd listen, anyway, wouldn't she? She'd at least listen. Wouldn't a woman listen to the only man that . . ."

"Listen? What'd you say to her? And suppose you could smooth over last night—after she'd bragged you up to him? What'll you say then? To hell with Pa? I'm my own man? You name it and I'll do it?"

"I—maybe."

"Not you, boy. Huh-uh."

"You wait!" I yelled. "Maybe I will."

I shook myself. It was like coming out of a bad dream and I felt kind of rested and eased. I brushed the water, rain, I guess it was, out of my eyes. I started running, and I ran the rest of the way home.

I stopped on the porch, and kicked the mud off my shoes. I wiped them solewards and sideways against the sacking Mary had laid out. I went into the kitchen.

"Well," said Pa. "What you doin' home?"

He was sitting down with his jeans' legs rolled up and his feet in a pan of water. He looked mighty sour. I figured he hadn't had such a good time bragging about Matthew Ontime getting his come-uppance.

"What you doin' home?" he repeated. "Why ain't you in school?"

I looked at Mary, but of course, there wasn't any help there. She looked like she was about to keel over herself.

"You get into some trouble? Is that it?"

"Y-yes, sir."

"They kicked you out?"

"What's the difference?" I said. "What difference does it make, Pa? We can't stay here on ten acres. We'll have to find a new place to crop, and . . ."

"They kicked you out. You got kicked out. I brought you up out of nothing, and pushed you up into something to be proud of, and now you've went and pushed yourself back. Almighty God writ His will as plain as day, an' you set yourself against it. You flouted *His* will."

"Pa," I said. "I couldn't help it. All I did was . . ."

"He gave me a stone, an' I was to bring bread in return. An' you set yourself against Him."

He held his hand out, and Mary scurried forward with a towel. He took one foot, then the other, out of the pan, drying them carefully, wiping between each toe. He got up, dropping the towel on the chair, and went into his bedroom. He came out with a long, thick harness strap.

"Face up to that wall," he said.

Mary moaned softly and threw her apron up over her face. Pa

shot her a glance, flexing the harness strap. He jerked his head at me.

"You better do what I tell you, boy," he said. "You better do it fast."

I had a mind to do it. He couldn't hurt me much more than I already was, and maybe it would give me the push away from him that I needed. Maybe it would take away the maybe about what I was going to say to Donna. If I got to see her.

But—

But I couldn't let him go ahead. It would be mean spite to let him, because I knew how he'd feel afterward when he found out the truth. I knew how bad he'd feel: If I was going to make a break, all right, but it was my job to make it. I couldn't spite him into making it for me.

"Pa," I said, "I didn't . . ."

"Face up there!"

"But I didn't."

His arm went up in a swift looping motion, and the harness strap zinged and popped. It whipped around my neck, and he jerked on it, and I went down. I toppled forward, going down on my hands and knees. The strap uncoiled and he swung it again.

And it did hurt. It always hurt. And this time it did something worse than hurt, something evil and sickening. And I knew I'd better stop him fast. It came to me that what I was feeling must be hate, and it sickened and scared me. Because despite all the put-on, I'd guess I'd never known what it meant to hate until then. Somehow I'd never learned how to hate.

And if it was like this, I didn't want to learn any more. I knew I hadn't better.

The strap came down on my back again—the third, the fourth time. And he swung it again. I started to get up, and he'd shifted ends; and the buckle whipped around my shoulders, nicking me in the corner of my mouth.

I stood up.

He looked at me, and he took a step backward, and his hand trembled when he pointed to the floor.

"Y-you better get down there, boy."

I started to shake my head. Then I nodded. "All right," I said, "if that's the way you want it."

"I seen it coming on. I seen you settin' yourself up . . ."

"Go ahead," I said. "Don't bother talking yourself into it. It ought to be easy for you by now."

"I"—he backed away another step. I guess he'd had to because I'd edged toward him. I'd done it without knowing it, my eyes fixed on his, the blood welling across my lips—"what's wrong with you, son?"

"Go ahead," I said. "Go on, Pa. You know what's wrong. Everything's wrong, and always was. That's how you get your exercise, takin' it out of me. Go on. What's the sense in stopping now?"

"I'm tellin' you, boy. You better . . ."

"Make me," I said. "Make me tell you, Pa."

He brought the strap up fast. It whistled and popped as he swung it up above his head. And I grinned at him, feeling the bad feeling that was now good to feel. It was like a coon must feel when a trap gets him, and he has to chew off a leg to get out.

I laughed, and the strap came down.

It fell from his hand to the floor.

"Tell me, Tom. I'm asking you to . . ."

I told him, watching what happened to his face, and for a little, I guess, it felt good. But I knew it wasn't good, so I stopped looking at him. I talked as fast as I could, and still make it clear, so's it would be

41

over with fast for him.

I finished, and he stood clenching and unclenching his hands, his head sagged lower than I'd ever seen it on his turkey-gobbler neck. Then he pushed it back, so's he could look at me, and his lips moved.

"That—that's just the way it was, son?"

"You know I wouldn't steal anything, Pa."

"No—what I meant—I mean you didn't tell 'em? You didn't tell 'em you—we—was hungry?"

"No," I said, "I didn't shame you, Pa. I just let 'em think I was a thief."

He nodded, and some of the pain went out of his face. It seemed to leap from his to mine. And I turned quickly, before he could see it, and went out the door.

I ran across the yard, ducking under the clothes lines, and into the old cowbarn that we used as a woodshed. I sat down on the chopping block and buried my face in my hands. And I tried to work up into tears. I tried as hard as I could, and the tears wouldn't come; and it was worse than learning what hate was.

I guess it's the worst thing there is when you lose everything you've lived by, and you can't even cry about it. Because it's not even worth that much, a single solitary tear.

And it never was.

I didn't look up when I heard him coming. He hesitated in the doorway—I knew he was there because he was between me and the light—and he cleared his throat. Then he came in, stumbling a little as he stepped over the lintel. And after a minute or two he put his hand on my shoulder.

"Tom," he said. "Tommy, boy . . ."

I moved my shoulder a little. His hand fell away.

His feet scuffled in the wood chips, and pretty soon I could sense the semi-darkness and I knew he was standing back in front of the door. He was staring off across the long broad fields, raising his eyes above the red clay soil to the horizon, looking across the fiery-red plains of Hell with its endless gauntlet of dead-brown imps—the cotton, the cotton, cotton, cotton—closing his eyes to them and see-ing only the horizon and its towering ranks of derricks. Steel giants, snorting and chuckling amongst themselves; sneering wonderingly at the cotton and the bent-backed pigmies amidst it. Huffing and puffing and belching up gold.

"Look, Tom," he said, softly. "Come an' look at 'em." And I stayed where I was.

"You hear me, boy?" he said. And I got up.

You do things out of habit. You keep on for a little while.

I went to the door and stood with him.

"Look at 'em," he whispered. "Just lookit that." Then he said, "Tuh-wenty-fi-uhv thousand dol-lars!" He said it just like the oil scout had said it. He repeated it a second time, and he started to do it a third. But his voice was dragging, and he gulped and swallowed midway of the twenty-five, and he didn't finish.

"God damn his eternal soul," he said.

And I said it after him.

"It's his fault! Everything's happened is his fault! He ain't fitten to live!"

"No," I said, "he isn't."

He started to look at me, but I reckon those oil derricks were a sight prettier; and habit was strong in him, too. Anyway, if he had an idea that we weren't goddamning the same person, he didn't show it.

Chapter Six

THERE'S NOT MUCH TO do by way of entertainment around a cropper's shack, even as nice a one, one that's actually two, as ours. And that's probably as it should be because, most of the year anyhow, you've got plenty to do outside. But sometimes it's kind of hard to bear, just sitting and not doing.

It's hard when you've got nothing to do but think—and you've got something to think with—and your thinking won't seem to lead anywhere.

We had an early supper, and Pa seemed a little out of himself. He didn't holler at Mary hardly at all, and a couple of times he passed dishes to me. And I guess that sounds like a pretty commonplace thing, but it wasn't with Pa. I couldn't remember when he'd ever done it before.

After supper he went over into the parlor and read the Bible for an hour or so, the Old Testament where most of the first-class curses are called down on people. He read to himself, he didn't speak out loud, I mean, but his lips kept moving with the words, and I could read them, too, just by watching him.

Finally, he closed the book and sat staring straight into the lamp flame. Then he sighed and took off his dime-store glasses and tucked them into the bib-pocket of his overalls.

"Guess I'll go to bed," he said. "Good time to catch up on my sleep these rainy nights."

I didn't say anything. His trying to make conversation took me by surprise.

"You don't need to though," he said. "Stay up as long as you want."

I guess he was surprised then himself, because he ducked his head suddenly and hurried out. He went across the breezeway and out on the porch, and he stayed there a minute or two—taking a leak, I suppose, to save a wet trip to the privy. Then he stamped back inside and his bedroom door slammed shut.

Mary looked across at me from the settee. "What's got into him?"

"Just trying to be decent," I said.

"Huh," she grunted, "he's got a sight of practicin' to do before he makes out. Mean ol' devil. You wait. I bet I fix him one of these days."

"Yeah?" I wasn't really listening to her. I couldn't imagine her fixing anyone unless she fainted and fell on 'em.

"You think I won't, but I betcha I do. I'll take the chop ax to him!"

"No," I said. "Don't even think that, Mary."

"Well . . . they's other ways. Bound to be some way of puttin' him in the hole."

I yawned and put my hand over my mouth. "Why do you stay on, Mary? He can't make you."

"Well, I . . . I . . ." Her eyes went sort of empty, and she began fumbling with the safety-pin at the neck of her dress. Her fingers moved faster and faster, and that was the only light in her eyes there was, the glint of a pin.

I'd asked her a pretty sorry question. You don't ask the dead why they don't get up and walk.

"Sho', now," I said, "listen to me talk! How in tall cane would I make out without you to do for me?"

"You"—she stopped fumbling with the pin. "I bet you'd really miss me, wouldn't you?"

"Why, you know I would," I said.

She blushed, as much as she could under the tan, and looked

pleased. And I thought, what about her? What'll happen to her if I pull out? And I figured it wouldn't make too much difference.

"Reckon I'll turn in myself," I said, and stood up. "How about you?"

"Might as well," she said.

I went over and kissed her on the cheek, and she held onto me a minute, brushing my hair back. She pressed herself against me, turning her head against my chest.

"Tommy . . . you want me to rub your back for you? I got some good chicken fat in the kitchen."

"It's all right," I said. "It doesn't hurt anymore."

"I don't mind. I jus' soon as not, Tommy. I like doin' things for you."

"It's all right," I said.

"I'd—I'd do m-most anything you asked me, Tommy. . . . You ask me somethin' an' see if I won't."

"Goodnight," I said, and I gave her a little slap on the bottom and went into my bedroom. I closed the door and sat down on the bed. And after a moment or two I realized I was holding my breath. I took my shoes off and stretched out, lying still to keep the cornshucks from rustling.

It was dark, there not being any windows. The only light came from the crack under the door. I heard her shoes creak, and the light all but vanished, and I knew she'd turned the wick down; just leaving the usual night-light in case someone had to get up. Then her door closed, and there was a soft *clump-clump* as her shoes came off. And her mattress creaked and rattled.

It rattled and rattled, and I lay still, almost not breathing. Then there was a little scraping thud against the partition, and she whispered.

"You asleep, Tommy?"

And:

"I can't hardly sleep at all. I just cain't sleep, Tommy."

And:

"Please, Tommy. You know. Whatchacallit. I been waitin' an' waitin' an' w-waitin' . . ."

I closed my eyes, wondering how Donna had probably seen it in her right from the first when I, right there with her every day, had to have it thrown at me before I could see it. And I guessed women could just naturally spot those things, because Mary'd sure tabbed the way Donna stood with me—I knew she must have—the first time she'd looked at her. That'd probably touched Mary off. That had been the sign she was waiting for. She was too beaten down to start anything, but once it was started she'd begun to move in.

"Tommy. . ." The thin planks squeaked as she pressed against them. "We could stay right where we are, Tommy, 'n do it 'n do it an' he couldn't catch us in a million years. Tommy"—she scratched against the wood—"take your knife, Tommy, an'—right here where I'm scratchin' you c'n . . ."

It must have been a couple hours before she gave up and went to sleep. She began to snore, but I lay where I was a little longer. I knew what I was going to do, but it was hard to get started. It was hard to break with habit.

Go against Pa? I ticked off that hold-back. I'd already gone against Pa, whether he knew it or not, and I was going to keep right on going.

The rain? I'd got rained on before, and I hadn't melted. Anyway, the rain had practically stopped.

How'd I get ahold of her? Well, I probably wouldn't catch her outside on a night like this, but I knew where her room was, in the downstairs south wing of the house. She'd told me one time, play-teasing, pretending like I could come and see her as well as not if I really wanted to.

Suppose some of the hired hands caught me, one of the riding bosses? Well, let 'em. Let 'em try something.

I eased my feet to the floor, and fumbled around until I found my shoes. I tied the laces together, swung them around my neck and stood up.

I got the door open, timing the squeak sound with one of Mary's snores. I closed it on another snore, and tiptoed across to the porch door. I got it open without any real racket, and ran crouching to the road. I wiped my feet on some wet weeds, hopping first on one foot, then the other. I put my shoes on and got going again.

Two miles is a pretty long hike on a muddy country road, but I seemed to make it in almost nothing flat.

I'd say, you name it and I'll do it, honey. You call me any dirty name you want to and I'll own up to it. I'll apologize to him. I'll let him punch me. You just point out the row, honey, and I'll hoe it. Heck, she wouldn't hold a grudge.

I came to the cottonwood grove and walked through it, just short of the end. Then I swung off to the right, taking cover where I could behind the trees and shrubs that skirted the lawn. I moved around parallel with the house until I came to a curving hedge that bordered the flower beds. I followed it in, crouching, toward the house, until I came to its end.

I hunkered down, staring at the windows of her room, so near and yet such a heck of a ways off.

I thought, "Come out, honey. *Please come out. Please, please come out, Donna.*"

I thought it as hard as I could, and it seemed like I saw something move at one of the windows. I could almost have sworn she was there and that she knew I was.

But I waited, and she didn't come. And I figured wishing wouldn't make her. So I picked up some gravel from the path and tucked it into my pocket, and I bellied down and crawled. I crawled under the shrub, and on to another one, the last cover, if you could call it that, between me and the house. I could toss the gravel from there, I reckoned. But I had to rest a minute first. All that duck-walking and crawling had run into time, and I was all out of breath.

I rested, stretched out on my stomach with my head on my arms, and I began to feel how wet I was; how soggy and smeared. I pushed myself up, shivering a little with the damp, and got to my feet. I stood bent over, trying to peer around the shrub; and like a cold wave hitting me, I seemed to freeze that way.

The hair crawled on the back of my neck. My stomach seemed to edge down toward my groin, and my chest squeezed around my lungs.

I stood real still. I couldn't bring myself to move. Then, I did move, I managed to turn around. And there he was, so close to me that I could've touched him—if I'd been of a mind to.

It was one of the riding bosses, a big breed they called Chief Sundown, though he wasn't a real chief, of course. He had a leather jacket pulled on over his undershirt, and a long black bullwhip was coiled over his shoulder.

Donna stood back of him and a little to one side, her white houserobe, or maybe it was what you call a dressing-gown—belted in tightly at the waist.

Chief Sundown shifted his glance a little, and she nodded to him. He moved back, sort of sinking into the shadow of the far shrub, and she moved forward.

"All right," she snapped, her eyes like black coals in the white-ash of her face, "what are you doing here?"

"W-hy"—I tried to smile, but my face was too stiff. "Why, I wanted to see you, Donna."

"You didn't need to sneak around here at night. You could have seen me today. I was there at noon and again this evening."

"But—well, I didn't think you'd be there! I didn't think you'd want to see me!"

"I see. But you thought I would tonight. Is that it?"

I tried to smile again. I was scared, and I could feel my temper coming up a little. But she was so close, and—and I wanted everything to be all right so much.

"Well?" she said. And I just shook my head, smiling. I could look down, and see the beginning swell of her breasts. I could see them, actually; the neck of her gown was open, and they began so high up. I could see past them, imagine past, because how can you forget or get over what's been part of you? I could see the flat stomach and the white, the cream-colored hips, flaring, swelling just enough; and I remember how warm and soft they'd been the night before when we'd ridden with my arms around them . . .

"Donna, honey," I said. "For God's sake . . ."

And I reached for her.

And she moved back, gripping the front of her gown. And back in the shadows there was a quick slithering sound.

My hands dropped down to my sides.

"I came here to tell you I was sorry," I said. "I was wrong. Pa was wrong. I'll do anything I can to make it up to you."

"You're appealing to the wrong person," she said. "After last night, I've stopped interfering in Dad's affairs. I've decided he's a much better judge of people than I am."

"Appealing?" I said. "I guess I don't . . ."

"Tell your Pa he'll have to see my father. Tell him that the influence, which you've doubtless boasted of having with me, no longer exists."

"But ..." I didn't get it for a minute, and when I did I was kind of stunned. The blood seemed to drain out of my face. "You mean— you mean you think I'd t-try to get you to . . ."

"Well," she hesitated, "you must admit . . ."

"I don't admit anything but what I've told you! I've been all mixed up and—an' I wanted to try and get straight again! But if you think I'd—I'd do *that*! You know I couldn't do that! Why, the one thing that's always bothered me is you having so much and—"

"Wait. Wait a minute, Tom!" She held up a hand. "I don't think we'd better talk any more tonight. This has been building up for a long time, and it's not something to be settled in the middle of the night behind a tree. I tried to see you twice today. I needed to see you. But you couldn't be bothered. You . . ."

"I told you . . ."

"You felt that you didn't have to. You could hurt me worse than I've ever been hurt, and then when you got good and ready you could come around and I'd fall into your arms. Wait! Perhaps you don't actually feel that way, but that's the way things have been and I think it's gone on long enough. "I"—she faltered—"I'm upset, Tom. I can't be fair to you now. I think you'd better go be-before I—Please, go. Quickly!"

"Sure, I will," I said. "Will I see you tomorrow, honey?"

"I—I d-don't know. I just can't . . ."

"The next day? There at the usual place?"

"I"—she shivered. "Oh, Tom, why did you . . ."

"I know. I know, honey. I'll be there every evening until you come, and you just take your time. But won't you . . . Send that breed away for a minute, honey."

"Well . . ." She sniffled, and looked over her shoulder. And my arms started to come up, because I didn't feel like I could wait another second.

Then her head snapped back around, and what I saw in her face I never want to see in another. Cold white sick. Burning-mad crazy sick.

But her voice was just a whisper.

"Breed," she whispered. "Breed."

I said, "Donna, honey, you know I . . ."

"It finally came out, didn't it?" She backed away. "You don't think much of breeds, do you?" She kept backing away. "That's why you came here, isn't it? To finish up the job. Why not? Red meat's cheap, isn't it? You know how cheap it is, don't you? You . . ."

"Donna!" I said. And I made a grab for her.

And she wasn't there.

But the Chief was. He was standing between us.

"Yes, ma'am?" he said, his eyes on me.

"M-make him go! Take him away! Run him away!"

"Yes, ma'am."

He put two fingers between his teeth and whistled, and back in the trees somewhere there was a nicker. It was one of the plantation's big bays. All their horses were bays. It came up to the chief and hung its head over his shoulder. He reached back and stroked its muzzle, never looking away from me.

"You understand me, Chief?"

"Yes, ma'am." He stepped back, and swung into the saddle.

"Run him, run him, *run him* . . . !"

"Yes, ma'am."

I backed up against the shrub. I started backing around it, pushing myself back into the branches. "Y-you try it! You try it, and by God I'll . . ."

The bull whip came off of his shoulder. He let it trail back behind him, then snapped the handle. And there was a *cr-aack* like a rifle going off. And a red hot iron seemed to jab through the toe of my shoe, searing clear up through my toes and into my ankle.

I'd known what was going to happen, and I'd set myself for it. I'd told myself I wouldn't jump or yell; I'd die before I did it. But I didn't die.

I jumped. I yelled.

I threw myself around the shrub, and the whip swung again, *cra-ack-cra-ack!*, and the hot iron jabbed me in the heels. I threw myself frontwards, and I got another load in the toes. I—

Backwards, *cra-ack-cra-ack!*, frontwards, *cra-ack-cra-ack!*, toes, *cra-ack!*, heels, *cra-ack!*

I leaped backwards away from the shrub, and I stumbled, went down sprawling on my shoulders, and the fire raced through my soles. I rolled over. I went into a running crawl, my eyes filling with blood, my insides pushing up into my throat and—

Cra-ack-cra-ack!, *cra-ack-cra-ack!*, left foot, right foot, left foot, right foot. *Cra-ack-cra-ack* . . .

I ran-crawled.

Cra-aack!

I screamed and ran, stumbling, blind . . .

Cra-aack!

I fell down, screaming, crawl-running, running, falling and rolling, and—

Cra-ack, cra-ack, cra-ack, crack . . .

Lights had come on. There was a blur of sounds, laughing, shouts, a scream, the same scream over and over. But they were just a blur like the lights. I couldn't really hear them. I couldn't really hear myself, what I was yelling. Everything had gone numb inside of me, and there wasn't any pain any more.

Or anything else.

I stood up. I turned around and faced him.

"Run me!" I yelled. "Try and make me run!"

Cra-ack, cra-ack!

"Go on! Run me, goddam . . ."

Cra-ack, cra-ack!

"—you! Run me! Try it, try it, tr . . ."

Crraaa-aaack! My ankle. I could feel the dime-sized spot of flesh leap away.

"Make me, make me, make me!"

Craaa-ack-a-craa-ack-a-craa-ack-a-craa-aack!

"Make me . . ."

"*Cra-*Tom, Tom Carver!"

"Try an' make . . ."

"Carver! Tom! Snap out of it, son!"

He was shaking me, a man with a bandage over one eye and a strip of courtplaster down his cheek. She was sagged against him, still and white, her head hung back over his arm. She couldn't see me run now, because her eyes were closed.

"Tom!" He was holding her with one arm and shaking me with the other. "Are you badly hurt, Tom?"

"Run me," I said.

"Come in with me. I want to talk to you. Will you do that, son? Will you come in with me, Tom? With Donna and me?"

"Run me," I said.

He hesitated. Then, he got his other arm under Donna's legs, and he lifted her. And her head hung back, eyes closed, and now she couldn't see me run.

"You should have known better than this, Chief."

"Yes, sir. But Miss Donna said to . . ."

"I know, I know," Matthew Ontime looked at me again. He tried again. "Now, listen to me, Tom—I don't know how this trouble arose, but I'm sure it can be adjusted. You were in a difficult position last night. I was in an unaccustomed one. My opinion of your foster-father isn't—well, we won't go into that. But as far as you and I are concerned — you and I and Donna, I'm sure, I'm more than willing to try to work something out that . . ."

Run me, run me.

I turned and hobbled off across the grass. And he said, "Take care of him, Chief," and I saw him going cater-corner toward the house, carrying Donna with her eyes closed so's she couldn't see me run.

The Chief touched my elbow, teetering along at my side in his high-heeled boots. "No hard feelings, boy? You ain't sore, are you?"

"You couldn't make me run," I said. "No one can make me run."

"No, sir, they sure can't. Ain't a chance in the world. So you just sit down here, now, and I'll get a car out and run you home."

"No one can run me . . ."

"Sure, but . . ."

I started running, running by myself because I wanted to, and the last I heard was, "No hard feelings, huh? No sense in . . ."

Chapter Seven

I DIDN'T RUN VERY far, just until I was in the grove and out of sight, until I'd showed 'em that they hadn't hurt me a bit. I fell against a tree, wrapping my arms around it; and I sank my teeth into the bark to keep from yelling. I hugged it, trying to ease the weight off my feet. Finally, I was able to let go, to stagger on to the next tree. And I got through the grove that way, moving from tree to tree.

I sat down on the edge of the ditch and scooted myself along sideways with my hands until I came to a little rain pool. I pushed my feet down into it, letting the water come up over my shoe tops and soak down inside.

I sat that way for quite a spell. It helped some, but I could tell my feet weren't ever going to soak free. They were swollen into the leather like sausage in a gut. I was glad I didn't have any socks on.

I swung around, facing the road, and pulled out the laces. Then I got a good grip on the toe and heel, braced myself and jerked.

And yelled.

I jerked and yelled and jerked and yelled. I kept jerking, because it looked like I might have waited too long as it was. Those were the only shoes I had, and I didn't want to have to dig them off with my knife.

I got them both off and put my feet back in the ditch. And they still ached like heck, and burned where the hide had come off. But the swelling started going out of them, and they felt a lot better than they had. I began to feel better, too. Some of the craziness seemed to go out of my head with the swelling.

I got up and hobbled toward home, walking in the mud as much as I could.

I tried to think back to the point I'd been at earlier in the evening.

I mean like, I'd done something pretty bad myself and they were entitled to pay me off. But I was a long way from feeling good enough to come around to that viewpoint.

Punching a man was one thing. It was something else to take a whip to him, making him cringe and crawl and scream in front of his—in front of a girl, and God knows how many other people. And, now, remembering the voices and the laughter, I reckoned quite a few others must have seen it.

That was a lot different. It was something you had to fan mighty hard to cool off.

So, I wasn't crazy any more. I could see that while I'd probably got a lot worse than I'd asked for, I had been asking for something. I could trace the fault back where it had started to Pa. He'd started it. They finished it. That was the right of the matter. But I could just see that, you know; only see it.

And until I could accept it, I knew it would be an awfully good idea for me to keep out of their way and them out of mine.

I had to sit down and rest several times, and it was just short of dawn when I got home. The stars were fading out and the man in the moon was down to a shadow of himself, and the cool-warm breeze that washes the path for the sun was rippling through the cotton stalks. The air had a sweet, clean-dirt smell. I couldn't hear a rain-crow anywhere. It looked like it could be a pretty nice day.

I got into the house and into my bedroom without anything happening. I undressed and wiped myself off with the inside of my clothes and tossed them under the bed. I laid out some clean clothes, and slid under the blankets and stretched out. And—

And Mary was shaking me.

"Tom! Wake up, now! Breakfast's ready and waitin'."

I tried to pull the covers over my head. It didn't feel like I'd hardly had time to close my eyes.

She kept shaking me. "Tom!"

"Don't want any breakfast," I said.

"Please, Tom! H-he's waitin' an' . . ."

"Since when did he wait on anyone?"

"Tom! You just *got* to! I don't know what to tell him, an' he'll . . ."

"All right," I said, "Get out and let me dress."

She left and I got up. I dressed, pulling on a pair of socks but leaving my shoes off. I walked out into the kitchen, making myself not limp.

He looked up at me over his saucer of coffee, then looked down into it again. "Woke up ahead of yourself, boy," he said, trying for a joke. "Plumb forgot your shoes."

"I didn't forget them" I said. "I'm going back to bed after breakfast."

I thought that would get a rise out of him, but he didn't seem to be in a rising mood. He couldn't believe what was happening; he'd had his own way too long. But he knew there'd been a big shift in the situation, and he was moving cautiously until he could shift his sights with it.

I sat down and put grits and biscuits on my plate. I broke the biscuits in two, poured sorghum on them and began to eat.

"Going back to bed, eh?" he said.

"That's right."

"How come?"

"How come not?"

I took a swallow of coffee, set the cup down, and looked at him steadily. He picked up his saucer again.

"Well . . . no reason, I guess. Reckon if you're tired, bed's the place for you."

"That's the way I figured it," I said.

I went on eating. He wanted to ask questions, let him ask 'em.

"You—uh—you got pretty upset about yesterday? Had a hard time goin' to sleep?"

I shrugged.

"Damn him," he said. "Damn his black soul to hell."

He finished breakfast gulping it down a little slower than usual. He got up, took down his hat and jumper from a wall peg and put them on. He pulled a straw out of the broom and tucked it into the corner of his mouth. He bobbled it up and down, looking partly out the door and partly at me, watching me out of the corner of his eyes.

"What'd you—what you think we'd better do, son?"

"What do I think?" I said. "You're asking *me* for advice?"

"Well, now . . ." He paused. "I thought—I was thinkin' you an' me'd kinda scamper around today and look for another place to crop. I was figurin' we'd better do that." He paused again. "Don't land somethin' pretty soon, they'll all be spoken for."

"That's right," I nodded.

"I thought we'd better do that, son. Awful late now, even, to be lookin'. People that ain't settin' tight from last year has already made their jump. Can't set on a place all winter, an' then move when the work starts."

"That's right," I said.

"You—uh—you gonna be through eatin' pretty soon?"

"When I get filled up. I'm eating while it's here to eat. I'm not doing any more digging after other people's leavings."

There was a crash, then the *ring-rattle-plop* a plate makes when it spins on the floor and falls face down. But Pa didn't say anything to Mary, or even look at her.

I heard her ease the plate off the floor and slide it into the dish-pan. I thought, *That's the way he'd like to have you. Yeah, and that's what you'd deserve. Anyone that's got feet to walk on and arms to swing has got it coming to 'em—if they let it.*

"But—uh—o' course," he was saying. "O' course, if you're . . ."

"That's right, too," I said. "I'm not going."

His head snapped around fast, and the broom straw fell out of his mouth. Our eyes met and held; and then he shifted back to the doorway.

"Damn him!" he gritted. "Damn his black half-breed heart. He ain't fitten to live!"

I poured myself more coffee, rattling and scraping the spoon in the cup as I stirred in the sugar.

"You ain't heard of anything have you, son? You ain't heard no one speak of a piece of land that might be open."

"Not a thing," I said. "Like you say, it's all spoken for by this time."

"Well, I guess I better—if a man looks hard enough . . ."

"Huh-uh." I shook my head. "There isn't any and no one's going to make a place for you. They don't want you around, understand? You're a good farmer, a lot better than the average. But no one wants a tenant who thinks he's God Almighty. Landlords don't need to pay a man to fuss and nag at 'em, and call 'em dirty names."

I saw his mouth twitch, and he started to turn his head again. But he wouldn't see the truth yet. He couldn't give up as long as there was anything to grab at.

"You're mighty upset, son. Don't know as I can rightly fault you much after the way they treated you at school."

"No," I said. "You can't fault me."

"Sure wish I could figure out what to do. Reckon I'll have to sell our ten here if I can't do anything else."

"To Matthew Ontime? You can't sell to anyone else. No one's going to buy a ten-acre plot inside another man's plantation. It'd cost him more to work than he could take out of it."

"But—damn him!" he yelled. "What am I gonna do, hey? A man's got to live!"

"I don't know," I said.

He brushed his mouth with the back of his hand, rubbing it back and forth. "You s'pose I could get a loan? The banks ought to make me a loan on it, hadn't they?"

"They probably would," I said. "They'd know they could turn it to Ontime when you defaulted."

"How—how much, son? They ought to treat me pretty good, anyways, hadn't they? It ain't just unimproved acreage."

"Yes, they'll treat you good," I said. "You might even get enough to—well, I wouldn't want to get your hopes up too high. I might be all wrong, but the way I see it, with all these improvements and all, you might get enough to, uh—uh—Oh, I kind of hate to name a figure. I'll probably set it too high, and then you'll be disappointed."

"No, I won't, Tom!" His buzzard's neck was almost tangent to his body. "I won't hold it agin you! Could I get enough to buy another place—a bigger one, maybe, that's run down."

"W-ell . . ."

"Enough to pay down on another place?"

"Well, now . . ."

"Tom! How much? You know about them things . . ."

"All right," I said. "You got enough now to ride until spring when you can draw against your crop—*if* you were going to have a crop. Say that you got your loan today, that'd leave you about six-seven months to go before the mortgage fell due and you had to move . . ."

"Yeah? So how much . . ."

"Just about enough to live through those months. Three or four hundred dollars."

"Three or—*three or four hundred!* B-but . . ."

"If you're lucky," I said.

And I got up and strolled back through the breezeway, and lay down again.

I waked up around noon when I smelled cornbread and black-eyed peas cooking. I'd slept soundly and I waked up to that smell and it was like I hadn't eaten in a week. The tension had eased out of me, and I felt starved.

My feet were in pretty good shape, about as good as they were apt to be in without a week or so's rest. I got my shoes on and went over into the kitchen.

I guess the way I'd stood up to Pa had taken Mary's mind off the way she'd carried on last night. Anyway, she didn't seem skittish or embarrassed; just half-scared—only half, since he was gone—and puzzled and sullen.

What was I trying to do? Why did I act like that? I kept it up, and Pa would be giving me what-for.

"Forget it," I said. "Let's talk about something pleasant."

"Like what, f'r instance?"

"Like that food. Or, better still, let's just eat it."

She didn't make a move to help me, so I took a plate from the shelf and went over to the stove. Then, she said, "Oh, I'll do it. You just set down, Tommy."

I said, "I'll get it," and I did.

I took my plate outside, along with a cup of coffee, and sat down on the edge of the porch.

She came out, too, a couple of minutes later. She hesitated, waiting I guess for an invitation to sit beside me. When she didn't get it, she went over and sat down against a post, her legs crossed in front of her on the porch. She crossed them one way, then another, smiling at me.

I went on eating. I was looking at the ground.

"You ain't mad at me, Tommy? I was just playin' about not getting' your dinner."

I shook my head, still looking down at the ground. I wasn't mad about the food, but I wasn't sure I wasn't going to be mad about something else.

"It's a real nice day, ain't it, Tommy? Too nice a day to be mad at anyone."

"Yeah," I said. "Ground's still a little damp though. Or maybe you hadn't noticed?"

"What's to notice about it?"

"Tracks. Footprints. When was she here?"

Her smile froze. "I—when was who here? Ain't nobody been here!"

I sat the cup inside my plate and put it down on the porch. I went over to her and caught her by the shoulders and jerked her up on her feet.

"When?"

"B-bout an hour ago. You was sleepin' so good, an' . . ."

"But you didn't tell her that. You told her I wasn't here, didn't you?"

She set her jaw, scared but stubborn. I gave her a good hard shake. I'd decided that I wasn't really mad about not seeing Donna. It was better, as I'd decided last night, if I didn't see her for a day or so.

But I still didn't like what Mary had done, even a little bit. I was through with having people take care of my business, and then tell me about it afterwards if they told me at all.

"Answer me! You told her I wasn't here?"

"I—all right, I did! You been in enough trouble without . . ."

"What did she say?"

"Nothin'."

"What did she say?" I tightened my grip. "What—did—she—say?"

"Tommy!" She gasped. "You're—lemme go, Tommy! She said she understood, that's all. She jus' said, 'I understand,' an' then she left."

"She didn't leave any message? Didn't say for me to meet her anywhere?"

"No-no—*Tommy!*"

I let loose of her. I figured she'd probably told the straight of things. Donna'd felt like she had to make a try at seeing me, but she'd realized, too, that it was probably a little too soon. She knew it, and I knew it.

But I sure did want her. I'd never wanted anything so much in my life. I was rested and half-way at ease in my mind for the first time in years, and I wanted . . .

"Y-you ain't mad, Tommy?"

"No," I said. "But understand me, Mary. Don't you ever, as long as I'm here, do a thing like this again. Do you understand?"

"As long as—you're not going away, Tommy! D-don't go . . ."

"I asked you if you understood me."

She looked up at me, her eyes searching my face. Then she nodded, smiling meekly. "Yes, Tommy," she said. "You know I'll do whatever you want."

I stepped back. All at once my hands were awfully sweaty. "Well," I said. "That's that."

"Tom-my." She smiled at me, smoothing the dress down over her breasts. Pulling it down. "Don't I always do what you want? Didn't I tell you I would?"

"I think I'll ..." I started to say I was going to lie down again, but I changed my mind. "I think I'll take a walk," I said.

"I'll go with you. It'll be real nice down there by . . ."

"I'm going out and sit by the road," I said, and I headed away from the porch fast, and I didn't look back.

I walked down the road a piece, stepped across the ditch and sat down on the bank. I turned my hands this way and that, looking at them, not really seeing anything, of course, but just to be doing something. I scraped a little skinned spot on one of my knuckles. I picked and tugged at the beginning of a hang-nail until I'd turned it into a real one. I wondered why a man's hands feel so empty at times.

Sometimes I've been out somewhere, walking across a field, maybe, and my hands will get that empty feeling, and I'll have to scoop up some clods or grab off a couple cotton bolls. I feel like I'll go crazy if I don't get something in my hands, just anything at all to hang onto.

I took my old knife out of my pocket, whetted it against the sole of my shoe and started whittling on a piece of stick. It wasn't much of a knife, wouldn't hold an edge much longer than a hog'll hold its breath, but it was something for my hands. I tried to think, more or less to keep from thinking about other things, what'd ever become of that pretty good knife I'd had.

I'd found it like I had this one—seems like if a man keeps his eyes open, he's almost bound to find a pocketknife lying in a field with rust all over it or aside of a fence, in the weeds, where someone's stooped to go under, or alongside a bush where someone's dropped his pants. There's all sorts of places you can find knives, and I'd found that pretty good one, like I'd found this one and every other one I've ever had. Only it didn't look like anything when I found it, any more than a penny's worth of pork chops.

But I'd took it home and scrubbed 'er up good with coal-oil; and I found a little piece of ash-wood for the side where the bone handle was broken off, and I carved and scraped it down and fitted it over the rivets where the bone had been and it went on slick as owl grease. You couldn't tell the bone from the wood side unless you looked real close; you couldn't tell then, unless you knew. I'd bet Nate Laverty a dime he couldn't tell, and sure enough he'd picked the wood side for bone. And I knew he didn't have a dime, any more'n I did, so Pete had been standing there and I carried the bet to him. And of course he knew, then, which side was wood and he picked it, so Nate didn't have to owe me a dime.

And then, somehow, I'd let it get away from me. And the heck of it was, I not only couldn't remember how I might have lost it but when I'd lost it.

You see I'd found this other old knife, meanwhile, I mean the knife I had now, and I'd been carrying it around to putter at when I had the time. And then one day at school it struck me that I had my good knife for quite a spell, so I looked for it high and low but I couldn't find a trace of it.

As near as I could recollect, I'd left it in a pair of dirty jeans when I'd changed to some clean ones; and, naturally, Mary'd chosen that day to wash. She claimed she hadn't seen anything of it, but that didn't mean too much. She always dumped her wash water in the privy to sweeten it, and she'd know that if she *had* forgot to turn my pockets out, the knife was long gone. So she wouldn't have wanted to own up to it. But I didn't know that was what had happened. I might have laid it down around the house, and she might have tossed it up on a shelf somewhere, not thinking about it. Or Pa might have picked it up and hid it on me, kept it in his room to use himself. Or it might have slipped down behind the seat in Donna's car when—well,

you know. Or . . .

I glanced up at the sun and gave a start. Then I had to laugh at myself. It was getting on toward evening. I'd spent almost the whole afternoon thinking about that blamed old knife!

Nate and Pete Laverty were coming down the road, joking and pushing each other. I stood up and brushed the grass off my pants, and went to meet them.

For a nineteen-year-old man, I've made a whale of a lot of mistakes. But I never made a bigger one than pushing that old knife out of my mind. If I'd done what I should have, I wouldn't have rested until I'd dug it up. I'd have taken the house apart board by board if I'd had to. I'd— But that was *if*, and you know how it goes.

If the dog hadn't stopped to scratch himself, he'd have caught the rabbit.

Chapter Eight

NATE SAID THEY HAD a note for me from Mr. Redbird, so I took it and pardoned myself to them and opened it up.

Dear Tom:

I have just finished a long talk with Miss Trumbull, and we both feel, as I am sure you will upon reflection, that you should and must return to school. Think, Tom! Despite almost over-whelming difficulties, of which I am more than aware, you have shown more promise than any other student. It has been a pleasure and a challenge to work with you. We have enjoyed four years of mutual respect, and, I hope, liking. Surely it is those years we must remember; not an unfortunate three or four minutes.

As you know, I was not responsible for Abe Toolate's employment. But I realize now that, being acquainted with his character all too well, I should have insisted on ending it—as I did successfully end it this morning. The situation was inevitably open to unpleasant interpretation.

I needed no proof of your honesty. Nonetheless, because it was the easiest way out, because I felt it necessary to appease a known thief, I asked you to tell me you were honest. Under the same circumstances, I might myself have said things I would later regret.

But don't think I'm letting you completely off, young man! I have a stack of Science 1 papers this high for you to grade, and I want the work done right, understand me? . . . As if you'd do it any other way.

I'll look for you in the morning, Tom.

Sincerely,

David Redbird

I finished reading, and tears were starting to come into my eyes. And I just didn't see how I could go back—right away, anyhow, until things were settled. But I could go and see him and Miss Trumbull, and . . .

I looked up.

Nate and Pete were grinning at me.

"What's so funny?" I said.

Pete snickered and gave Nate a nudge. "Looks pretty lively, don't he? Couldn't hardly tell he'd been out dancin' all night."

"Yeah," said Nate, and I could see the orneriness sticking out of him and Pete. They were like that, slow to pick up a grudge. They'd swallow something and spit it up at you later. "Yeah," he said, "but he's a pretty lively fella. Got a sweater to keep him hotted up."

"Now look," I said. "I told you yesterday that I spoke out of turn. What . . ."

"Kind of spoke a little out last night, too, didn't you?"

"What do you mean?" I said. But I knew, of course. The whole town, everyone at school, was probably laughing about me.

"How's your feet?" said Nate. "How they feel, big boy?"

They busted out laughing, haw-hawing in my face; and I tried to laugh with them, but it wasn't any good.

"Look at 'im!" Pete haw-hawed. "Looks like he's been chawin' persimmons!"

"Chawin' grass, that's what he done!" cackled Nate. "Fella, why'nt you tell us how them feet . . ."

That was as far as he got, because just about that time I whaled off and kicked him on the chin. And Pete made a dive for me and I kicked him, too.

They went white and silent, their chests slumping with the pain. Then they both made for me at once, and I slammed them both. I gave them each a short stiff-arm, my fists doubled. And they grunted and went down in the road. They staggered to their feet, waving their arms wildly, and I slammed them again. I knocked them down in the road a second time, and a third—and that trip they stayed down.

I tore up Mr. Redbird's letter and threw it down on top of them. I stared at them, panting, hoping they'd razz me just a little bit more—praying to God that they wouldn't. Because I didn't want to stomp them to death, and I knew I would if they said anything.

They didn't. Maybe they couldn't, or maybe they were afraid to. Anyway, they just lay there, their faces as yellowish white as their meal-sack shirts. And I turned and walked away from there fast.

I almost ran toward the house. I went into my bedroom, slamming the door, and threw myself down on the bed. I shivered. My head felt hot as fire, but I couldn't stop shaking. It was like I had fever and chills. I thought, *I've had enough. No one else better pull anything.*

I hammered my fists against the mattress. I wished now that I'd given Nate and Pete a real punching. That was what I needed—to pull the anger and shame out of myself and pass it on to someone else. Now, though, it was all corked up inside of me, and . . .

"Tom"—Mary's hand closed over my forearm and turned me on my side. "What's the matter, Tommy?"

"Go away," I said.

"I ain't going 'way till you tell me."

"You'd better," I said. "You'd better go away fast, Mary."

"Why?" She said it *why-ee?*, teasing-like, and sat down on the edge of the bed. Her hip was almost against my face, and I could smell her—the musky, wanting-it smell. "Why-ee, Tommy?"

I sat up and gave her a push. But she was sitting solid. She was a lot more steady than I was; and I guess I didn't push very hard. She was something to strike back at, you see. Or strike with. It seemed like if I did it to her, I'd be getting back at them.

70

"You'd better go," I said. "Pa'll be here pretty soon."

"Huh-uh."

"I'm telling you, Mary. If you don't get out of here, I'll—I'll ..."

"Yes?" And she dragged it out, *yes-ss?*

I lay back down on the pillows. I'd told her, hadn't I? I'd told her and all the others, but they wouldn't leave me alone. Now I was through talking.

She stood up, smiling at me. She kept on smiling, never taking her eyes away from mine, as she stepped out of first one shoe then the other.

She pulled her dress down over one shoulder. She eased the other arm out of its sleeve, then slid the dress down past her hips and stepped out of it. There wasn't anything on underneath.

She'd had it all planned, got herself all ready, before she'd come into my room.

"Move over, Tommy," she said. And I moved over.

"Now," she said. And she stretched out by me. And . . .

Up until then she'd been all smiling and cool and sure of herself. But then her arms went around me, and her body swung in against mine. And if there was ever a crazy woman, she was it.

All at once, all at the same time, she was laughing and crying and giggling and sobbing, biting and clawing and petting at me. And I don't mind admitting I was scared as all heck. I forgot all about myself, how sick-angry I'd been. All I could think of was getting away from her; but it was too late then, of course.

And after that first minute I stopped wanting to get away.

It didn't last much longer than a minute. Then she fell back on the pillows, her body heaving and quivering like she'd run ten miles.

I pushed myself up on my knees and slid off the bed. And I wasn't breathing so easy myself.

Five seconds before, I couldn't have been dragged away from her. Now I felt like I'd gag and start puking if she so much as laid a hand on me.

She was smiling again, narrow-eyed, trying to pull me back to her with her eyes.

"Tommy . . . That was good, wasn't it?"

"Get up and get dressed, Mary," I said. "Come on. Start moving."

"You like better'n her? Say you do, Tommy, an' I'll get up."

"Suit yourself about what you do," I said. "Stay there and let Pa find you."

"Wait, Tommy! Let's . . ."

But I didn't wait. I walked out of the room and out of the house, I drew a fresh bucket of water from the well and sloshed it over my head and face. Then I dried myself on the porch towel and combed my hair and sat down on the edge of the porch.

I heard Mary clomping around in the kitchen, building up the supper fire. It began to get dark and she lit the lamp; and I could smell the coffee coming to a boil. But she didn't come out and she didn't call to me.

I almost wished she would because I was beginning to get hungry, and I'd've asked for a biscuit or something if she'd given me an opening. But she didn't, so I stayed where I was and kept quiet myself.

Around true-dark, six o'clock or so, Pa turned in the gate from the road. He nodded to me, and I nodded back. He stepped to the kitchen door, told Mary to hurry up the supper and splashed water into the wash basin.

He washed, and sat down on the porch beside me. After a minute or two, he cleared his throat and spoke.

"Didn't have much luck at the banks, son. Kinda like you said it'd be."

I didn't say anything. He hesitated, then cleared his throat again.

"Heard you—uh—There's talk around that you had some trouble last night."

"That's right," I said.

"You shouldn't've gone up there by yourself, son. You ought to've told me what you had in mind and prepared yourself right. I'd've been plumb proud to go with you."

I turned and looked at him, frowning, not getting what he meant. Then it came to me; he thought I'd been aiming to do Matthew Ontime some dirt.

I started to set him straight. But just then Mary called out that supper was ready, so I let it ride. I was hungry, and, after all, what difference did it make to me what he thought?

We all sat down at the table. Pa gulped his food whole, as usual.

He finished eating ahead of the rest of us and refilled his coffee cup. I felt him squinting at me over the rim of his saucer; then, without looking, I knew he was staring at Mary. Her fork rattled against her plate and he went on staring. Finally she scooted back her chair and headed for the stove with the biscuit pan.

I looked up at last. He still had his eyes on her. She was standing at the stove, her back to the table—waiting for him to look the other way. In the dim light of the lamp, I could see her shoulders trembling. And yet she was standing straighter, less beat down than she usually did.

Pa lowered his saucer to the table. "What are you doin' over there?" he said—softly but his voice seemed to ring through the room. "You makin' them biscuits?"

"No-no, sir."

"Bring 'em here! You hear me, Mary?"

"Ye-yes, sir."

She turned around and came slowly toward the table, the pan trembling in her fingers. She started to sit down.

Pa kicked back his chair, grabbed her by wrist and jerked her erect. I stood up; and he pulled her toward him, staring into her face.

"What's the matter with you?" he said.

"Nothin'." She actually tossed her head a little. "What's the matter with *you?*"

He gave her a yank that almost jerked her off her feet. She let out a little moan and that was the end of her defiance. She folded up like a weed at sundown.

"I ain't done nothin', Pa! Y-you lemme go, now! I . . ."

"I been watchin' you," he said, slowly. "I seen you prissin' around all through supper, squirmin' and flauntin' your backside an' turnin' all red an' rosy like . . ."

"I ain't neither!" She ducked her head and began to cry.

"I m-mean—it a-ain't really like that."

Pa let go of her arm. He threw it away from him, letting it strike against her breasts. And she moaned again.

"Y-you're always w-watchin' me! You get me all upset with y-your watchin' and then when I do somethin' outta nervousness, y-you fault me about it!"

"Well"—Pa hesitated, and some of the hardness went out of his face. "Well, maybe."

"Y-you know you do! I can't turn around w-without y-you . . ."

"Maybe," Pa repeated. "Just maybe. An' I'm gonna keep right on watchin', you hear? An' I better not never see nothin' like—like I don't want to see. An' I don't want no more of your lip, regardless, you hear?"

She nodded shakily, edging backwards away from him. As scared as she was, it looked like she might back right on through the stove and out the wall.

I stepped between the two of them.

"She hasn't done anything," I said. "Why do you keep badgering her?"

"I know what I'm doin', son."

"So do I," I said, "and I don't like it."

His eyes widened, blazed for a second. Then the fire died out of them, and he turned slowly and started for the door. "I'm tired," he said. "Everything's falling to pieces an' I can't put it together again. I'm too old, too tired . . . I—I think we better talk a little, son."

"Maybe we had," I said, and I followed him out of the house.

Chapter Nine

HE SAT DOWN ON the lintel of the woodshed, and I sat down aside of him. Not close; as far away as I could get. He noticed it and sighed heavily, like you sigh when you're asking for sympathy. He reached behind him and picked up a sliver of kindling. His hand went into his pocket, then came out empty; and he tossed away the sliver. Either he didn't have a knife with him, or he'd changed his mind about whittling.

"About Mary," he said. "I reckon you think I'm pretty hard on her?"

I shrugged.

"I got to be hard on her, son. You see . . . Well, you've probably wondered—maybe you've wondered about her. How a widower was able to adopt a young girl. Well"—he swallowed and went on dog-gedly—"I didn't adopt her. I took her. I just took her out of the place she was in, an' they didn't dare put up a fuss about it. An' she didn't. They seen the wrath of God was in me, an' they didn't stand in my way . . ."

I waited. He sighed again, but not so fakey as he had the first time.

"Now you're gonna say that she was awfully young," he said. "She was young, an' maybe she was there against her will or she didn't know no better. But that ain't the way it was, son. She was doin' it because she liked to. She was—she was just a—just a hole. That was all she'd ever been from the time she was old enough to walk, an' that's what she'd still be if I hadn't got hold of her an' put the fear of the Lord in her."

I still waited. He moved uneasily on the lintel.

"So—so that's the way it is, son. That's why I got to keep bearin' down on her . . . You"—he paused—"Now maybe you think it's odd I'd pick up someone like that to look after you; but I knew I could keep her in hand, an' it was the Lord's work to take her away from that house of sin. You see that, don't you?"

"No," I said. "That isn't what I see."

"Well, now . . ."

"You took her to punish her. She was built with a certain appetite—some women are. And you fixed it so she could never have what she needed to satisfy it. You've starved her, punished her, for almost twenty years. Do you want me to tell you why?"

It seemed funny, the way that everything fell into place in a matter of seconds. But I guess it wasn't really so strange. He'd kept me bowed down as much as he had her. Until the last day or so, I'd never got a good look at him.

"You're dead wrong, son. Y-you—why would I—?"

"You got her out of a whore house," I said. "How did you happen to find her? What were you doing there?"

"I—son, you know I never ..."

"You never have since, no," I said. "Because you were punishing her. You held her responsible for something that happened to you, and you've made her suffer for it. That's the way it was, wasn't it?"

"She—do we got to talk about it, son?"

"You started it," I said.

"Yeah," he nodded, heavily. "So I guess . . . I guess . . . It was the end of pickin', Tom, an' I'd gone into town to get my pay from the gin. An' I'd got a late start, kinda, because your—because Effie, my wife, was sick an' I couldn't find no one to set with her. An' by the time I got my money from the gin the stores was all closed, and I couldn't get the needfuls I was s'posed to take home. I—I guess I should have gone home without 'em an' come back the next day. But it was a long walk, an' I was afraid of highjackers with all that money, so . . ."

"What was wrong with your wife?" I said.

"Huh?" he started. "Oh, nothin'. Nothin' you'd understand, son. Some kind of female complaint."

"I see," I said.

"So, like I was sayin', I decided to stay the night in town. An', well, I had had a few drinks. I drank a little in those days. I wasn't really drunk, you understand, but . . ."

"Yes," I said. "You were drunk."

And he hesitated and said, "Yes, I was drunk. You can fault me for that—for not knowin' what I was doin'. Because I honest didn't know, son. I was lookin' for a boarding-house, some place to sleep. An' I seen her an' asked her where there was one, an' she promised to take me to a place. An'—well, you know where she took me."

I nodded. "That takes care of the night, when you were drunk. But you were sober the next morning."

"Yes," he said. "I was sober."

"But you didn't go home?"

"I didn't go home," he said. "I couldn't make myself, somehow. I stayed there for a week, an' my money was gone, more'n seven hundred dollars. An' I could've kept on stayin', far as she was concerned, because she'd do it for nothing, being like she was. But the house wouldn't stand for that, an'—an' she'd wrung me dry. So I went home. I—son, you just can't understand! I . . ."

"Go on," I said.

"My wife was dead. Been dead for four days. One of the neighbors'd come in an' was takin' care of you. But . . ."

"How old was I?"

"Oh, six-seven months, I reckon, but . . ."

"No," I said. "I'd just been born."

I heard the creak of his jaws as his mouth dropped open. He put his head down in his hands and held it there a moment. And then he raised it again, staring off across the fields toward the twinkling lights in the drilling rigs.

"Well, son?"

"Well?" I said.

"It's been mighty hard for me, boy, not bein' able to claim you for my own son. But you see why I couldn't, don't you? I couldn't let you know I'd—that I'd . . ."

"That you'd let my mother die in childbirth while you slept with a whore for a week?"

"Tom . . . Try to understand, boy . . ."

I laughed. "What makes you think I don't understand? It's taken me a long time to get around to it, but I understand everything about you, Pa."

"I don't ..."

"No," I said, "you don't. Or you won't let yourself. You won't see yourself as you are. You made one big mistake—a bad one. But you can't come out and admit that you really made it. You've got to lay it all on to Mary; you've got to make her do the suffering. You're not actually sorry for what you did, because you've never admitted that you did it. It was her fault—yes, and mine. For being born. I was the cause of my mother's death, and . . ."

"Son!" He grabbed me by the shoulder. "I don't think nothin' like that! That ain't . . ."

"Let go of me," I said.

"But you . . ."

"Let go of me."

He let go.

"Maybe you don't see it quite that way," I went on. "But I'm not far wrong. You've proved that I'm not. You didn't need to tell me the whole truth to let me know that I was your son. There's only one reason why you didn't let me know. Because you could get more out of me, make me feel that I owed my life to you for taking me in."

"Son"—he shook his head curtly. "You're makin' me out to be mighty low-down."

"Because you are," I said. "Because I can't help myself. Every time I've slipped a little, wavered a little from what you thought I ought to be, you've taken it out on my hide. And I've let you get away with it, because I felt that I had to. You'd taken me in out of charity, so I had to take whatever you handed out and be grateful for it."

He was still shaking his head. He'd been shaking it all the time I was talking.

"I done plenty for you," he said, "an' don't you say I haven't. Maybe I ain't been too easy-goin', but easy-go don't make the mare run. I've made you make somethin' of yourself."

"Like what?" I said. "Like getting kicked out of school because I was starved down to eating scraps? Like making me knock a man down who wanted to help me?"

"I done plenty," he repeated.

"All right," I said. "You've done plenty. But I'm not giving you a chance to do any more."

I stood up, brushing at the seat of my pants. He stood up, too, bending his head back on his neck to look up at me.

"Now," he said, "I suppose you're fixin' to walk out on me. I try to be honest with you an' tell you the truth, an' ..."

"I was going to do it, anyway," I said. "You've just helped me to make up my mind."

"Where you figure on goin'?"

"I don't know."

"You mean you don't want to tell me? You're cuttin' out of touch with me for all time?"

"I mean I don't know," I said. "But I'm cutting clear of you for good, yes."

"When?"

"In the morning, probably."

"Don't go, Tom."

He raised a hand toward me, then let it drop trembling at his side. "Maybe I been all wrong about everything, but I sure didn't aim to be. An' whatever I done it was because I wanted you to be somethin' better than I was. I . . ."

"I know," I said. "I was your redemption. I was your way of squaring yourself with the Lord. I was supposed to be you, what you wanted to be. I wasn't entitled to have a life of my own."

"I said, maybe I was wrong, son. B-but"—his voice was begging —"ain't I done—I still done plenty, Tom. I pointed out the path of the righteous to you, an' I kept you on it. I . . ."

"Are you sure," I said, "about that?"

Years before, right after we'd moved to Oklahoma, Nate and Pete and I had been walking home from school together; and we'd come to a place along the road where the county was putting in a new culvert. And there was a rat crouched back in the angle of a pile of bricks, and we'd got ourselves some sticks and moved in on it.

It'd tried to run between our feet, and we'd driven it back. And it'd darted along one angle of the bricks, then the other; and we'd kept moving in closer. And finally it was squeezed clear back in the corner, with no way of going farther back, and no way out in front. And what happened then, well, it gave me bad dreams for a month afterwards.

It wasn't a real big rat. But all of a sudden it reared up on its hind legs and it looked as big as a dog. And it seemed to have about a million teeth, and every one of 'em showing. It came out of that corner in a kind of running waltz, waving its front paws, all those teeth chattering against each other. And that was the end of Mr. Cornered Rat; it was us that was cornered from then on. We had the whole world behind us, but it didn't seem like there was any room at all. We fell all over each other trying to get away. And I think we were lucky to get away without a bad bite.

But—

But that had been a long time ago, and a man forgets things he doesn't like to remember. Or, remembering, he goes right ahead and does the same thing all over again. He figures he'll be luckier than he was the first time, or he's mad and doesn't care. He thinks he's got nothing to lose, that he's been pushed down as far as he can go. And he's wrong, of course. There's always something worse that can happen to you.

Pa was reaching for me again. Sticking his hand out toward me, and holding it back at the same time.

"What you mean, son?" he was saying. "What you mean, am I sure about—about . . ."

"You know," I said. I grinned at him. "You noticed it at supper. I had her, Pa. Just like you."

"No!" he said. "No, you didn't! S-she wouldn't dare. She knows what I'd do if . . ."

"But it was me," I lied. "I made her. Oh, she took to it fast enough after we got started, but I *got* her started. She didn't have anything to do with it, and you can't fault her for it."

He wagged his head, moving it slowly from side to side. "That ain't the truth, son," he said quietly. "You're saying it to spite me."

"How?" I said. "How would that spite you?"

"You want to take all the meanin' away. You don't want to leave me nothin'. I ain't got nothin' left but that, an' now—now . . ."

"Now you haven't got that," I said. "Ask Mary. She'll tell you the same thing I have." *Naturally. She'd be afraid to tell him anything else.* "Got anything more on your mind before I turn in?"

"You didn't do it, son! Say you didn't do it."

"I did it," I said.

He stood blinking at me, his chin wobbling like he was trying to swallow something that wouldn't go down. Then suddenly he turned his head and spat, drawing the back of his hand across his mouth.

"All right," he said.

"Just all right?" I grinned. "You don't want to make something of it? Take the strap or maybe the shotgun to me?"

"No," he said, and there wasn't anything in his voice at all. It was like he'd written the word on paper and handed it to me. "No, that wouldn't be bad enough."

I laughed, and way off somewhere in the backbrush a loon picked up the laugh and tossed it back across the fields. *Hee-ah, whoee!, hee-ah, whoee!* And I shivered in spite of myself. And Pa nodded gently.

"The Lord will punish you," he said.

Chapter Ten

MARY WAS STILL IN the kitchen when I passed through, but she heard Pa plodding along behind me, so she kept busy at the dishes and didn't speak. I crossed the breezeway and went into my bedroom.

I took off my shoes, and opened the door a crack. I listened, pretty uneasily, glad of what I'd done to Pa but a little worried about Mary. I told myself that he wouldn't do anything. I'd taken all the blame. He'd be afraid she might turn on him, like I had, and walk out. And—I thought—if he did give her a tongue-lashing, it wouldn't scare her any more than she already was and she had it coming. That, and then some. Because I could see now that she'd never really done anything for me. Everything she'd done had been aimed at tying me to her so she could use me as soon as I could be used. She couldn't help it, I reckoned, any more than a skunk can help stinking. But that didn't make the smell any better.

I listened, and I couldn't hear a thing out of the way. I could hear their voices now and then, not words just voices. I could her the creak of shoes on the planking. Then, finally, I heard the kitchen door close and the door to Pa's bedroom, and I figured that any minute she'd be coming across the breezeway.

But ten, twenty minutes passed and she didn't come.

I got uneasier and uneasier. I wondered if Pa had been mean enough to send her packing without even letting her take some clothes.

I tiptoed out of the bedroom and opened the outside door. I looked out, around the yard and down the road; and I couldn't see a sign of her.

I closed the door again, wondering what the heck had

happened—what I'd better do. And, then, because I couldn't think of anything else, I tiptoed across the breezeway and into the kitchen.

I listened a minute, and that was all that was necessary. It was more than enough to know that I didn't need to worry about Mary.

I came back across the breezeway, not bothering to tiptoe; because the noise that mattress was making, they wouldn't have heard me if I'd stomped. And they wouldn't care that I'd heard them. It wasn't in Mary to care. It wasn't in Pa either now that, as he saw it, he'd lost his last chance at redemption.

He was damned through me. Now the bars were down and nothing mattered to him.

I undressed and stretched out on the bed, and my stomach felt all queasy and tight; I felt like any minute I might throw up my guts. I thought about that afternoon—about Mary and me that afternoon—and I wondered if I could ever scrub away the dirt that seemed to be on me. I scratched and scrubbed at myself, thinking about her. And suddenly I sat up, shamed, the blood rushing to my face.

Shamed and sick. For them, for myself.

I lay down again. I sat up and lay down again. I closed my eyes and the image of them came into my brain.

It must have been two or three hours before I finally dozed off.

Just like always, the breakfast smells awoke me in the morning. And I was out of bed and pulling on my pants before I remembered that this morning wasn't like the others. I hesitated, almost of a notion to walk right out from my bedroom without looking at them again. But I figured that might suit them too well, so I decided against it.

They were sitting at the table, eating, and there wasn't any chair or plate at the place where I always sat. Pa looked at me, looking without looking, like I wasn't there; then bent back over his food. Mary gave me one quick glance, then dropped her eyes.

She'd never been able to meet anyone's eyes for long, and she couldn't now. She was still beat down. But she wasn't beat down too much to let me know with that glance exactly how she felt about me. She didn't need me now; I was in the way and the quicker I got out the better.

See? her eyes said. Tried to do me dirt, didn't you, and it didn't work. Now you better watch out.

I sauntered over to the cupboard, and took down a plate and cup. I took a knife, fork and spoon from the drawer and set my own place at the table. I dragged up a chair and sat down.

Mary gave me another one of those glances. I winked at her. I leaned forward, pulled the food dishes up in front of me and loaded my plate. I filled my coffee cup and began eating.

I didn't pay any more attention to them than they did to me, from then on. Just looked right through them when I bothered to look up at all. And, of course, they had a head start on me, but, at that, it seemed like they finished eating pretty fast.

Pa pushed back his chair and got up. Mary got up, too, as if she'd been waiting for him to move; and they went out on the porch together.

A couple of minutes after that I heard a car drive into the yard. The door slammed—two doors; a couple of men were getting out. I stopped eating.

I'd been pretty hungry, everything considered, but all at once I couldn't have put down another bite if I'd been paid a million dollars. I went all-over stiff and cold and dead. It was almost as if I knew what was going to happen.

I stood up; something seemed to pull me up from my chair. I

walked out the door and onto the porch.

Pa and Mary were out in the yard, and there were two men with them. And when I came out, they all turned and looked at me; and then they started for the porch together. The two men in front—Sheriff Blunden and one of his deputies.

"Howdy there, boy," the sheriff said. "Wanta talk to you."

"Talk to me?" I said. "Talk to *me*?"

"Yeah, and I want you to talk to me. Talk plenty and straight, understand, boy?"

The deputy hunkered down in the yard on his boot-heels; squatting just short of the porch with his Stetson pushed back and his fingers already working on a cigarette. Blunden sat down on the porch, facing me, with his back to a post. He was short and fat, a man who liked to take it easy—and the way I must have looked, he probably thought he could. Up until the last year he'd run a cotton gin.

"Where's your knife, boy?" he said, and his voice wasn't unfriendly. He waited, and when I didn't answer—I still couldn't speak—he asked the question again.

I began to come to a little. I took my knife out of my pocket and held it out to him.

He shook his head.

"I mean your other knife. Pretty knife with bone on one side the handle and ashwood on the other."

"I haven't got it anymore," I said. "I lost it."

"Where?"

"I don't know. Somewhere around the house, I think."

He shifted his eyes sidewise a second, then moved them back to me. "Seen bigger houses," he said. "Shouldn't be too much trouble to find it in there."

"I didn't say I'd lost it there," I said. "I said . . ."

"I heard what you said. When'd you lose it?"

"I don't know."

"Don't know when you lost a pretty knife like that? Didn't mean any more to you that you can't remember a-tall?"

"Well," I hesitated. "I think it was about a month or so ago. I can't say for sure because I had this other one to use, and the other— the one you're talking about—may have been lost a while before I discovered it."

He took off his hat—it was just a plain store hat like business people wear—and fanned himself with it. "Hot," he said. "Don't know when I seen it so warm this time of year. You recollect a fall like this, Bud?"—he glanced at the deputy.

"Not in the last ten year," the deputy nodded. "No, I'd say it was all of twelve year. Had a tol'able warm November back in . . ."

The sheriff grunted and put his hat back on. "Now, let's see, boy," he said. "Let's see—uh—mmm—ain't you been having quite a little trouble lately?"

"Well, I—I don't know," I said.

"Don't know? Don't know where you lost your knife, don't know when you lost it, don't know whether you've had any trouble. Don't know—or you don't want to talk?"

"Look," I said, "what's this all about? I don't know what you're getting at."

"Got caught stealing, didn't you? Up at the school?"

"No, I didn't!" I said.

"Cussed out your teachers?"

"No, I"—I hesitated—"I said a thing or two I shouldn't have, but I didn't mean anything by it. I was just out of temper, kind of an' . . ."

"Temper," he said. "Don't know anything that'll get a man in trouble quicker. Reckon you was kind of out of temper when you knocked down Matthew Ontime, weren't you?"

"No," I said. "I was just scared on Pa—his account." I jerked my head at Pa without looking at him. "They'd been having an argument, and Mr. Ontime got sore and I was afraid he was going to ride him down."

"Didn't seem to me like he was," Pa put in, mildly. "The way I looked at it, he was just through talking and was gonna ride away."

I gasped and choked up. The sheriff said, "Well, that's a young'un for you. Don't mean no harm at heart, prob'ly; just can't keep off the half-cock. Can't keep their hands in their pockets and their tongues in their heads. Why, I recollect . . ."

"Now, wait a minute!" I said. "See here, now! Can't you see he's lying to you? I didn't have anything against Mr. Ontime. I wouldn't ever have gone near the place except for *him*!"

"Yeah?" Blunden nodded. "Your Pa drag you up there night before last?"

"I"—I stopped.

"Uh-huh," he said. "Your Pa tell you to go around calling—'scuse me, miss—Mr. Ontime a dirty son-of-a-bitch, boasting about what you were going to do to him?"

"I didn't do that," I said. I spoke before I remembered that I had done it.

"You didn't? I can name you a couple of boys, friends of your'n, that'll say you're a liar."

"Well, maybe I did," I said. "I guess maybe I did. But I didn't really mean it."

"Half-cocked," he nodded again. "Yessir, that's the whole trouble with these young'uns. . . . Now, you was up there to the Ontime place and you got chased off with a bull-whip; took a real toe-popping. How'd that set with you?"

"I didn't like it," I said.

"No, sir, don't reckon you did. Wouldn't have liked it myself, even if I got it from a white man. When'd you say you had that knife of yours last?"

"I didn't say. Look, Mr. Blunden, maybe if you'll tell me . . ."

"I heard you had it yesterday. A couple of fellows say they saw you whittling with it."

"It was this one they saw," I said, "and they really didn't see it. All they saw was me whittling. I had the knife put away by the time they got to me."

"Had a little ruckus with 'em, I hear. Or maybe they're mistaken about that, too?"

"We had one," I said.

"Didn't like their teasin', huh? Still pretty sore about that bull-whipping."

"I didn't like it, no," I said. "I didn't like the whipping. But I guess I had it coming."

"Where were you last night, say, around midnight?"

"Where—why, I was right here," I said. "I was in bed at midnight, and the rest of the night, too."

He eased one flank up off the porch and reached his hand into his pocket. He brought it out again and there was my knife, the one I'd lost.

"At midnight last night," he said, "Matthew Ontime was murdered. Someone stabbed him to death with this knife and tossed him into one of his own hogpens, and what was left of him when they found him this morning wasn't pretty to see. It took someone with a pretty bad grudge to do that. Now, if you can prove you ain't that someone I'll prob'ly be just as happy as you are."

Prove it? Prove I hadn't killed him? I laughed, puzzled and

irritated, like you will when something doesn't make sense.

"That strike you as bein' funny, boy?"

"Well, gosh," I said. "I mean—well, that's crazy, Mr. Blunden. I wouldn't—why, anyone ought to know I wouldn't . . ."

He sat looking at me, waiting, as if he didn't see anything unreasonable about it at all. And the deputy was looking at me the same way. And Mary and Pa . . . Mary and Pa. Pa.

And a Cadillac pulled into the yard, and Donna got out of it. Her face was all drawn and white and hard, and she stood at the side of the car, watching me. Waiting for me to prove *that*, that I hadn't done it!

The sheriff glanced at Pa. "You said he was out of the house last night, Mr. Carver?"

"We-ell," Pa dragged it out. "No, that ain't what I said, sheriff. I said he could have been without me knowing about it, like he was the night before."

"What about you, young lady? You say you sleep over in that end of the house."

"Don't ask me." Mary ducked her head. "He could sneak in an' out all the time for all I know."

"And y-you you know I never did!" I stuttered over the words. "Both of you know it! I was never out of the house but the one night, night before last, and that was to try to square things with Mr. Ontime. Tell 'em, Donna!"

She didn't answer me. She stood off there in the yard, like she didn't want to get close to me. "That's why he said he came," she said.

And they all looked at me again.

"Well, boy?"

"Ask them where they were at midnight." I pointed at Pa and Mary. "This all started as his quarrel. I got dragged into it through him."

"I know where they were," said the sheriff. "Miss Mary had to step out to the, uh, commode about that time. Your Pa heard her when she came back in, and called out to her. Seems like that takes care of them pretty well."

"They're lying," I said.

"Reckon so? You weren't in bed asleep then?"

"Sure, I was! What's that . . . ?"

"Then how you know they're lying?"

He waited; and there didn't seem to be much that I could say. What good would it do to say that they'd slept together? What would it get me and how could I prove it?

"Guess you'd better come along with us, boy. Want to get your hat or somethin'?"

"Well," I said, "I guess maybe I—I better . . ."

I suppose I looked pretty dazed and bewildered, and I was. But not so much because of what had happened as what I intended to do. It didn't seem like I could do it; it seemed like I was planning it for another guy. But there wasn't any other guy—it was me that was trapped. And I could only see this one way out.

Still, it was hard to get started.

I wondered why they didn't see what I had to do and try to stop me.

"Well, you better get movin' then," the sheriff said. "Go on, or we'll have to go without it."

"Yes, sir," I said.

And I didn't linger after that.

I went through the kitchen door, lifted the shotgun off its hooks, and went right across the breezeway into the other end of the house. Moving fast, walking light. The door there was off the latch and I eased it open without a sound. I stepped back into the room, then ran—I hit the screen in a running jump.

I landed in the yard, threw an arm around Donna and whirled her around in front of me. I held her with the one arm and leveled the shotgun with the other.

"N-now," I panted, "now you bastards. On your feet!"

Chapter Eleven

THEY GOT UP, SLOWLY, like people in a dream; and Mary's face was so sickish gray I laughed out loud. I jerked the gun at the deputy, drawing my arm so tight round Donna's breasts that she gasped.

"You, Bud," I said, "raise your hands, turn around and back toward me." I said it like I'd been saying things like that all my life, and he did exactly what I said. "Now unfasten that gun belt with your left hand—keep the other one up!—and let it drop. Good! Now, get back there with the others."

He moved forward again. I hooked my toe under the belt and booted it under the porch.

"Boy"—the sheriff found his voice at last. Up until then no one had spoken. "You don't want to do nothin' like this, boy. This won't settle nothin'. You just . . ."

I triggered one barrel of the shotgun; and there was a hell of a kick because I could only cradle it in one arm. But I head on, and the right rear tire of his car exploded.

"All right," I said, "all of you start walking. Stick close together and head for that field."

"Tom . . ." It was Pa. "Maybe I made a ... Sheriff, wouldn't it fix things if I was to say . . ."

I swung the gun on him. I rubbed my finger along the trigger. I tightened it. And his face was fish-white with fear, but to me it was red. I was seeing everything through a gauzy, hate-red curtain.

Fix things? *Fix things?* He'd killed my mother; he'd taken her away from me. He'd taken Donna away from me. He'd taken nineteen years of my life—and now he was taking the rest of it. And now . . .

Now—*I was laughing, laughing and crying, and silent, my eyes frozen on his buzzard's head*—now he was going to fix things!

I'm not sure why I didn't blast him all over the yard. Probably because it would have been too clean and quick for him. Because I knew there'd be another time and a better way to pay him off.

"You made a mistake," I said, "but I'll do the fixing. Count on that, Pa. I'll be back to do some fixing. I won't forget you. I won't forget her. That's a promise and I always keep my promises."

I let it soak in on him, grinning at that fish-white pallor of fear. Then I moved backwards toward the Cadillac, pulling Donna with me.

"Walk, damn you!" I yelled. "Head for that field or I'll give you the other barrel!"

They walked. Fast. Mary was dragging her feet a little, but she couldn't help it.

I slid under the wheel of the Cadillac, holding Donna so that she was half outside and half in. I got it backed into the road, tossed the gun into the back seat, and yanked Donna over the wheel and into the seat beside me.

I pinned one arm up behind her, so that she couldn't move without breaking it. I turned the wheel with the other hand, and headed down the road. But I just couldn't do it very long. About a mile down the road, where there weren't any houses nearby, I stopped the car and let go of her arm.

"I'm sorry I had to do this," I said. "You can get out here."

She opened the door and started to get out. She didn't speak or look at me.

"Donna!" I said. "Wait . . ."

She waited.

"Back there," I said. "You said you didn't know. And I know how you feel—how things look to you—but you must know I . . ."

"I didn't know," she said, "but I know now."

She got out without looking at me, and started up the road. I sat unmoving for a second. Then I slammed the car into gear and stepped on the gas. And I whipped by her so close that the fender grazed her. But she didn't waver an inch or a step.

I glanced up into the mirror, and she was still walking just like she had been. Moving in a straight line with her shoulders squared and her head held high.

I didn't look back after that.

I slowed down for the county road, wondering which way I'd better turn. I had less than a third of a tank of gas, and no money. And I knew I wasn't going to use that shotgun to hold someone up. Anyway, there'd be an alarm out for me in thirty minutes or less—just as soon as someone could get to the Ontime place and telephone. I'd never be able to make a getaway in this car.

An idea came to me. Not a very good one, but there just couldn't be any very good ones in a spot like this.

I turned the car toward town.

I had to slow down at the school, because someone had kicked a football into the road and a couple of guys had run out and were scrambling for it. They got out of the way, finally, and I went on past. And they waved and yelled at me.

"Hey, Tom! Where'd you get that baby?"

"How about a ride, Tom?"

I waved, and stepped on the gas.

Just then the schoolbell rang and I knew it was five minutes until nine.

The town was laid out in a series of squares, like most county seats are. I turned at the first square, the outside one that is, angling around it to the other side of town. I hit the main road there, followed it for about a half-mile and turned off again. Another quarter-mile, and the side-road I was on dipped down to a railroad crossing.

I pulled the car off into the weeds and got out.

It was a spur-line road that ran into Muskogee, and there was a train due by on it at nine-thirty—about twenty minutes from now, as I reckoned. This far out of town, it would be going too fast for me to catch. With the tracks down in a cut this way, I couldn't have made the run for it that I would have needed to make.

But they wouldn't know that, I hoped. It would look like I'd caught it.

I walked down to the tracks, stepped up on one of them, and walked foot in front of foot, east toward the trestle across the creek. And, no, it wasn't hard to do for anyone that'd walked a furrow as much as I had. It was about a hundred yards to the trestle; and, being below the fields, I got there without being seen. I wasn't any too soon. The tracks were humming. The train was highballing out of town, whistling for the crossing behind me. I turned side-wise to the tracks, and jumped into the creek.

I knew it was about five feet deep in the middle, which was more than enough to break my jump. But I'd overlooked the fact that the bed was bound to build up around the trestle joists. I came down in about five inches of water, just enough to cover the sloped up sand, and one foot went down each side of the slope. The jar snapped my head back, then down against my chest. My ankles socked down into the sand and bent under me.

I yelled out with the pain. I hurt so bad that it was all I could do to pull myself under the trestle when the train passed over.

I wrapped my arms around a joist and hung on, yelling as the train shook it, making my legs shake. I was sure that my ankles were broken. All I could think of right then was that I'd have to let go, and that they'd find me trapped there in the sand with my head under water.

But I didn't let go, badly as I wanted to, and after a while I could feel something in my ankles besides the pain; the sugary numbness began to go out of them. I wiggled and pulled them out of the sand, one at a time. I tested them with my weight. I yelped a little when I did it, but I *could* do it. There weren't any broken bones.

I worked my way from one joist to another, until I was in the shallows near the opposite bank. Then, I left the trestle and headed up stream. This way, of course, I wouldn't leave any trail for dogs to follow. The creek ran between steep wooded banks, the tree branches curving over it and sheltering it; so, if anyone was out in the fields, they wouldn't see me.

The creek swung south and east. I could follow it for about ten miles until it petered out in the hill country. Then I'd take to the hills. There wouldn't be any people there, since the land couldn't be farmed and the blackjack and scruboak wasn't worth cutting. So I'd go on through the hills to the Kiamichi River, steal a boat and drift south.

Down to Texas, maybe. Over to Arkansas, maybe.

Somewhere. I'd figure it out when the time came.

Right now I had ten miles of creek to walk. That was job a-plenty for me to work on.

The shallows kept curving down, making me walk with my weight thrown sideways on my ankles. Branches and bushes poked out from the stream banks, and I had to keep dodging under them or moving out into the water around them.

By the time I was a couple of hundred yards from the trestle, I was winded and pain was running up and down my legs in a way I didn't like to think about.

I rested a little while, hanging on to an overhead branch to ease the weight from my feet. I went on again, plodding through the water and sand and pebbles. A strong cold wind was working up, rattling and shaking the trees. I tried to walk faster, hoping my body heat would dry me.

I had pretty good going for the next half-hour or so. The stream curved sharply in and out, cutting away the banks until the shoreline was flat instead of sloping. I must have covered all of a mile without having to stop and rest.

Then I hit a bad stretch, a really bad one.

It started with an overhang that was so low and bush-covered that I had to duck-walk to get under it. I finally worked my way through it, and there right ahead of me was a real poser: an arrow-shaped wedge of land that poked out about ten feet into the stream. It was covered with thorn bushes.

I eased forward until I was facing it, then started to walk around it sideways. I got around to the point of the arrow, flopping my arms to keep my balance. Then my feet shot out from under me, and I went down in about eight feet of water.

I came up and I grabbed those bushes, thorns or no thorns. I pulled myself around the wedge, and got to a little sandy flat where I could sit down. I took out my old knife and began digging out the thorns, so doggone mad and upset that it's a wonder I didn't whack a finger off.

And right up above me—not more than twenty feet away, it sounded like—a man hollered:

"Hi, fella! Where you think you're headin'?"

I went stiff as a board and the knife dropped from my hands. There wasn't any place to run down here, and I couldn't run anyway. It was all I could do to walk. I turned my head slowly, opening my mouth to call back to him—because the news would be all over this end of the county by now, and he probably meant business.

Then he spoke again, and he was quite a distance away now. He'd moved back into the field, and I could only make out a few words of what he was saying:

"Reckon you're . . . the news . . . ?"

". . . damned shame"—another man's voice—"hard to . . ."

I let out my breath. My heart was pounding like a Model-T with the bearings burned out.

The first man, I reckoned, had been up there in the brush setting a snare probably, when he'd spotted a friend cutting crossfields. I listened, trying to hear what they were saying.

". . . care if . . . Indian. Fine a . . . a real gentleman and I'll . . ."

"Well . . . catch him, all . . ."

". . . nut the bastard!"

I got up and took to the creek again.

They all had their minds made up. Now it was just a matter of catching me and nutting me: sentencing me to the chair. I thought, *I wished I'd brought that shotgun. I'd do a little nutting myself.*

I made it another mile or so, and then I just caved in entirely. I was blue with cold. My ankles felt like chunks of ice with hot wires running through them. I fell face forward on a stretch of sand, another place where the bank had washed out. After a few minutes I got up enough strength to roll up into the weeds and pull them around me. I rubbed myself with them. A little sunlight drifted down through the trees, and it helped a lot. Some of the chill began to leave me.

Now, I thought, it's time to do some thinking. Real honest to gosh thinking. So far you've just been running, and—

I went to sleep.

I waked up to the smell of smoke and cooking corn, and it was all so much like the way I was used to waking that I thought I was home. I lay there smiling for a second, thinking I was sure going to have to do some work on that roof. I started to sit up and my whole body seemed to have been starched stiff. And I remembered where I was. Then I plopped back down in the weeds. Because I hadn't dreamed that smell of smoke and corn. That was real.

The fire was on the other shore, down in a wash almost opposite where I lay, and there was an iron pot boiling on it. Seated around it in a half circle was a dozen Indians. Full bloods. The old oldtimers who wore store clothes but still kept their hair in braids. They were having some kind of ceremony, I guessed.

I watched them, peering through the weeds. I couldn't leave

until they did. After a few minutes, one of the old men got up and dipped a piece of bark into the pot. He brought it out, covered with something white, and licked it. He grunted a word or two in Creek language to the others. They all got up and began dipping into the pot, grunting and gesturing.

It was *pashofa*, corn fixed something like hominy, and they acted like it was pretty good. They ate steadily for all of a half hour, and I watched with my mouth watering. I hoped they'd leave the pot when they left, but I was pretty sure they wouldn't. Indians always clean up good after themselves. At any rate, I didn't see how I could get across to scrape it if they did leave it.

Everyone except the man at the pot—the medicine man, I guess—stooped over the creek. And each of them got himself a little rock or pebble. They laid them down in a pile on the sand; then two of them walked back up into the bushes and disappeared.

Nothing happened after that for maybe two or three minutes. They all just sat silent, still as statues. Then the bushes started rattling and rustling again, and the two Indians returned, pushing another man ahead of them.

His ankles were hobbled and his hands were bound to his sides. His chin was bowed down against his chest. The medicine man began grunting at him, faster and sharper, and slowly, like he could hardly bear to do it, the man brought his head up.

It was Abe Toolate.

Chapter Twelve

EVEN STANDING IN THE shadows, and at the distance I was from him, he looked pale. He was just about the scaredest-looking man, white or Indian, I'd ever seen. His lips moved, like he was about to say something, and he sure shouldn't have done that, it seemed, because the medicine man began shrieking at him; and the two Indians at his side threw him down on the ground.

He lay on his back, with the wind knocked out of him, maybe. Anyway, he didn't move or try to speak again.

The semi-circle spread out. The medicine man took two clam-shells from his pockets, and handed them to the Indians nearest him. They passed them on, to the men nearest them, and those two passed them on again. They moved from man to man, until they reached the two men sitting next to the creek.

One of them made a pass at the creek, making out like he was filling the shell with water, but not actually doing it. He started it back up the line again; and the Indian opposite him waited a minute, then went through the same motions and passed his shell back.

The medicine man squatted down at Abe's side. He grabbed him by the nose and forced his mouth open. One of the shells had reached him by this time, and he snatched it and "emptied" it down Abe's throat and handed it down the line again. Then he took the other shell and "emptied" it into Abe and passed it back. He reached for the first one again.

It went on and on, the shells moving at just the right speed to keep the "water" pouring down Abe's throat. And I knew they weren't actually doing it—only going through the motions—but it all seemed so real that I found my breath coming hard. It was as though I were being executed by drowning in the old tribal way, as they were "executing" Abe.

The medicine man stood up, and put the clamshells back in his pocket. He walked to the pot, scooped out some *pashofa* on a strip of bark and carried it back to Abe. He offered it to him, pushing it out at him then jerking it back. And Abe stood up—somehow, in all the goings-on, his bonds had been untied. But he didn't touch the *pashofa*, of course.

Dead men don't eat.

The medicine man laid the bark strip on the sand. He squatted over and reached for the pebbles which the others had gathered. And the others drew in their semi-circle until Abe was standing outside of it.

The medicine man covered the bark with the pebbles, laying them over it one by one—making a tiny stone *wickiup*. That *wickiup* was Abe's grave. The bark was his body.

Everyone stood up again in that tight semi-circle, and Abe was shut off from sight. Then the semi-circle broke up, and they began scraping out the pot. The execution and burial were over, and they got ready to leave.

But Abe was already gone. He'd vanished while they'd turned their backs on him. And I wasn't any Indian, of course, but I knew that what had happened to him—though he hadn't been harmed physically—was about the worst thing that could happen to a man.

A few years ago, during a smallpox epidemic, an Indian died up in the old Osage Nation. The doctors pronounced him dead, and all his kinfolks and friends came to his house and began mourning. And he wasn't really dead—just in a state of coma—and all the racket snapped him out of it. He sat up in bed and asked them what the heck was going on. And no one heard him—no one would admit hearing. They just got up and walked out.

From that day on, as far as the Osages were concerned, he didn't exist. He'd "died" and the dead don't come back to life. No one would speak to him. He'd try to stop them on the street, and they'd just look right through him and keep on going.

He was one of the wealthiest men in Oklahoma—had all sorts of oil holdings. And when he really did die, of loneliness, I guess, there was a big turnout for his funeral. But not a single Osage came. To the Osages, all his kin and friends, and anyone he cared anything about, he'd been dead for years . . .

And Abe Toolate would be dead from now on. To all the full-bloods, and all the part-bloods who came under their influence. Practically every Creek of any degree. They wouldn't be told what he had done to be "executed"—the old full-bloods would keep that a secret. Otherwise, the white men would take over Abe's punish-ment; and the old Indians preferred their own brand of justice. They wouldn't side with the whites against their own kind.

But the part-bloods wouldn't need to know why he'd been "executed." They'd know that it wouldn't have been done without a darned good reason, that they'd better steer clear of him and let him stay "dead."

I watched the Indians leave, walk up through the bushes and disappear, dragging the *pashofa* pot with them. And I wondered what the heck Abe *had* done, anyway, and how the old men had found out about it. Of course, they had ways of finding out things—nothing much happened that they didn't know about. And, of course, Abe had been bringing disgrace on the tribe for years; stealing, lying, getting drunk. Probably, I decided, they'd just let everything pile up and then paid him off for the lot by "killing" him.

I sat up, pushing the whole matter out of my mind. I tried to stand up and my legs crumpled under me. I looked down at the water and shivered. I knew if I tried to walk in that creek another ten feet, I'd just fall over on my face and never get up.

I looked up through the trees, trying to estimate the time of day. I figured it would be all of two hours until dark; and I'd have to wait until it was dark.

I took off my shoes, and began chafing my feet and legs. I scrubbed and pounded them with my knuckles, and they started aching like anything; but the blood came back into 'em and they felt warmer. I stood up and began stamping them into the weeds, flapping my arms at the same time. Then I rested a little and started in all over again. Something told me I'd better if I wanted to keep on living. And I did want to.

I hadn't been kidding when I'd warned Pa that I'd be to see him. I was going to live long enough to do that if I never lived any longer.

I concentrated on him, thinking of how, as soon as they gave up looking for me, I'd go back. I'd go back at night, or, early in the morning, say. I'd stay in the woodshed until they got up—I'd wait until they had the fire going and were sitting down to breakfast. Then I'd take the axe, I'd have it sharpened up good by that time, and sneak across the yard.

I'd creep up on the porch, not making a noise, and—and then I'd move in front of the door. And they'd raise their eyes, real slow. And I'd grin at them. Grin and twirl the axe, and bring it back over my shoulder.

I was going to do it. I knew it—like you sometimes do know things—and I knew it was going to be exactly like I was planning.

It got dark.

I crawled and pulled my way up the slope to the field above. I rested a few minutes, then started back toward the trestle.

It wasn't nearly as far back as I'd thought, but if it had been much farther I couldn't have made it.

I crawled across the trestle on my hands and knees and tumbled into the cut on the other side. I lay there for a while—I think I must have passed out for a few minutes. I crawled up the slope of the cut and under the fence. I got my hands on top of a fence post, pulled myself up and staggered across the field.

It was a dark night, and that was good, of course. But it made walking twice as hard as it would have been. I kept stumbling and going down, and each time it was a little harder to get up. I didn't seem to have any joints in my legs or ankles. I had to push myself up, kind of from the hips, and along toward the last I was plopping down on my face a half dozen times or so before I could make it.

I got to the fence on the other end of the field, crawled under it and pulled myself up again. And I was sure glad she lived on the edge of town. I was glad she had this orchard.

I stumbled and staggered through it, pulling myself along by the trees. I went across the yard at a staggering run and fell down on the back steps.

I pounded on them and she—and Miss Trumbull came out.

"Why, what in the—Oh, my goodness!" she said. "Oh, heavens to Betsy!"

And I passed out again.

Chapter Thirteen

WHEN I CAME TO I was sitting at the kitchen table, and she was trying to pour coffee down me. I choked and coughed, and she pulled the cup away. Then she put it back to my mouth again, and I swallowed it down without stopping.

"Well!" she said. "That's better, isn't it?"

"Yes, ma'am," I said.

"Of all the foolish—Well! I won't say anything *now!* Can you walk?"

"I—think so," I said.

"Let me help you. Now, lean on me, you stubborn thing! There. This way, now. I've got a nice hot bath all ready for you."

We went up the stairs with her arm around me, and she guided me into the bathroom. She pushed me down on a stool, steadying me until she was sure I wouldn't topple off.

"Feeling any stronger?" she said. "Think you can undress yourself?"

"Yes, ma'am," I said, though I wasn't feeling too strong. "Sure, I can."

"Do it then. The quicker you're in that tub the better. I'll go get you a . . ."

She went out, leaving the door open. She came back carrying a nightgown, and I hadn't taken off but one shoe.

"I think this will fit you," she said, hanging the gown over a hook. "It belonged to my father, God rest his soul, but—Why aren't you out of those clothes!"

"Well, I—I thought I'd better wait," I said.

"But . . . Oh, my goodness!" she said. "Oh, heavens to Betsy!"

And she hurried out, slamming the door.

I undressed and got into the tub; and I'd never been in a real bathtub before but I did it easy as pie. I lay back in the water, soaking, letting the warmth sink into me. And I guess there aren't many things nicer than getting warm after you've been cold a long time.

I scooted down until the water came clear up to my chin. I closed my eyes, and—

And there was a banging at the door.

"Thomas! Thomas Carver! Have you gone to sleep in there?"

"No, ma'am," I said. "I'm getting right out, Miss Trumbull."

"Well, shake a leg. And be sure to dry good before you put on that nightgown. You don't want pneumonia, do you?"

"No, ma'am," I said.

"Humph!" she said. "Probably do. Wouldn't surprise me a bit."

She was waiting outside the door when I came out. She took me into a room adjoining the bath, jerked down the covers of a big four-poster and motioned. I climbed into it.

"Now, leave those covers down," she said, when I started to pull them up. "I'm going to rub your chest and—No, you'd better take these pills first."

I took the pills, quinine they tasted like, and she began rubbing my chest with some strong smelly stuff. She finished rubbing, spread a thick flannel cloth over it and buttoned the neck of the gown.

"There, that'll fix you," she said. "Now, can you eat anything?"

"Almost anything," I said.

"How about some nice roast beef?"

"Well, I—I reckon that'd be fine," I said.

She frowned a little. "You don't like roast beef?"

And I didn't seem too feverish any more, but I could feel my face turning red. "I don't hardly know," I said. "I never ate any."

She hurried out of the room and down the stairs, and I heard her slamming things around in the kitchen. I lay back on the pillows, feeling warm and good in spite of what I had on my mind. Everything seemed so clean and peaceful, lying there listening to her; humming, singing a few words now and then:

In the sweet bye and bye,
Hmmm-hmm-hmm,
We will meet on that beautiful shore.
Hmmm-hmm-hmm.
In the sweet . . .

She came back up the stairs, walking slow, and when she came into my room I saw why. She was carrying a tray that must have been five feet around, and it was so loaded with food you couldn't see between the dishes. There was a big plate of roast beef—and I knew I'd like it fine—and brown potatoes and creamed corn and greens and a big piece of apple pie and coffee and—

I pushed myself up in bed and started reaching for the tray before I remembered my manners.

She placed it in my lap and stood back, her eyeglasses twinkling and sparkling in the light.

"How do you feel, Thomas?"

"Fine," I said. And I picked up a fork and laid it down again. "Still pretty weak, but—"

"You'll be stronger after you eat. Now, you're welcome here, you understand that. I know you, and I know you couldn't have done that terrible thing; and I don't need you to tell me you didn't. But if you think you *would* feel like talking tonight . . ."

"I'll feel like it," I said. "I can talk right now. Anything you want to know."

"No. You eat while your food is hot. At any rate, I want you to talk to Mr. Redbird as well as me. I want to have him come over."

"Oh," I said, and I frowned. "Well, I—I don't know about that, Miss Trumbull."

"Thomas. Don't you know who your friends are, by now?"

"Yes, ma'am," I said. "I just don't see much point to it. All I want to do is get myself pulled together, so that I can . . ."

"No, sir!" she said. "No, sir-ee, that is not all you want to do. Thus far you're not guilty of anything but a bit of rash conduct. Foolishness. The . . ."

"That's not the way it looks, though. It looks like I'm guilty as all-getout and I can't prove I'm not."

"Oh, yes, you can," she said firmly. "But you've got to face up to the situation. You can't accomplish anything by running. Now, I want to ask Mr. Redbird over, Thomas. He'll know more about what to do than I will."

"Well," I said, "if that's what you want, I reckon that's what you'll do."

"Thomas . . ." She shook her head sadly.

And I figured I must seem pretty curt and ungrateful.

"I'm sorry, Miss Trumbull," I said. "I'd like to talk to Mr. Redbird. I really would."

"Fine!" she said. "Splendid. I'll just give him a ring, and—what's the matter?"

"The telephone," I said. "I imagine you're on a party line, and ..."

"Oh . . ." She hesitated. "Well, of course, I wouldn't need to say why I wanted to see him, but—Perhaps you're right. I'll just run over to his house. It'll only take a few minutes."

"I sure hate to put you out," I said.

"Fiddlesticks!" she said. "Stop saying sure all the time. Stop saying reckon. Haven't I taught you anything at all? Eat your dinner!"

"Yes, ma'am," I grinned, and I got busy.

I heard the front door close as she left, and that beef was sure—certainly good, but I stopped chewing for a minute. I had a notion that I was doing the wrong thing by letting her get Mr. Redbird. But it was just a notion—not even a real Grade-A hunch; and after what I'd been through, I was apt to be jumpy without any reason. So I shrugged it off and went back to eating.

I was just finishing up about a half-hour later, when I heard them coming up the front steps and across the porch. The door opened and closed, and she called up the stairs:

"Thomas? Everything all right?"

"Yes, ma'am," I called back. "I su—certainly am."

"I'll get more coffee for all of us," she said. "You go right on up, Mr. Redbird."

He came up, and I felt a little funny, embarrassed; and, of course, I didn't need to. He winked at me, pushing me back on the pillows when I started to get up. He laid a hand on my forehead, puffing his pipe thoughtfully, his eyes warm and friendly.

"Think you might live?" He smiled, and sat down.

"Yes, sir. I hope so," I said.

"Just don't worry," he said. "Everything's going to be all right."

Miss Trumbull came in. She set the coffee tray down on a stand, lifted the other one onto the dresser and poured coffee all around.

"Now," she said, seating herself in a straight chair and nodding to me. "Now, Thomas!"

I started talking.

I told them everything there was to tell. The only things I kind of glided over was how much Donna had meant to me and the messy way Mary had acted. But I could see that they understood without having all the details.

I finished talking. Miss Trumbull looked at Mr. Redbird.

He sat frowning a little, tapping the stem of his pipe against his teeth.

"You think, then," he said, at last, "that your father did it?"

"I'm sure he did," I said.

"Just to put you in a bad light? I don't know, Tom; the risk he'd run and all. It seems like a rather extreme measure to me."

"I'd call it a little more than putting me in a bad light," I said, trying not to make it sound too short. "He was killing me—the same as killing me. And Mary would have told him about Donna, and he was fixing me there, too. Just wiping me out wasn't enough for him. He wanted to make her hate . . ."

"Mmm, yes, I suppose." He didn't seem very convinced. "Can you think of any other reason why he would have killed Mr. Ontime?"

"Well," I said, "there's the oil. He may have thought that with Mr.

Ontime out of the way, Donna would lease their land for drilling and he could lease his."

"I'll just bet that was it!" said Miss Trumbull.

But Mr. Redbird shook his head.

"I'm afraid not. There's a basic contradiction there. If he'd simply killed Matthew Ontime, yes. But to kill him and frame Tom for the murder, that doesn't add up. He'd know that Donna would hardly be inclined to accommodate the father of the man who had killed her father."

"Well . . ." Miss Trumbull hesitated.

"Well," I said, "I know I didn't do it."

"Now, Tom," Mr. Redbird smiled, "keep your nightshirt on. Of course," he added; "we mustn't overlook the big thing, your father's hatred for Mr. Ontime. In itself, it would hardly be sufficient to move him—to prompt him to take such a terrible risk—but when you couple that hatred with his hatred for you . . ."

"And he felt like he didn't have anything to lose," I pointed out. "All that was left to him was getting even with me and Mr. Ontime."

"Yes," he said. "Yes, that's true. But still . . ."

He paused and frowned down into the bowl of his pipe.

"Let me ask you this," he said. "Is there a chance that your father went up to the plantation to argue with Mr. Ontime?"

"No," I said, "he wouldn't have done that. He was too stiff-necked. Anyhow he'd have known it wouldn't get him a thing—unless it was what I got."

"I'll tell you why I ask, Tom. You see—well," he frowned troubledly, "it all seems very clear-cut in a way. Your father hated you and Ontime. He had your knife, and he had Mary to alibi for him. So he committed the murder; q.e.d. With premeditation . . ."

"You're doggone right he did," I said.

"Perhaps. It seems that he must have. But the premeditation—and it's there axiomatically—bothers me. Mr. Ontime worked long hours, but it would be extremely unusual for him or any of his employees to be out and around the place as late as midnight. Your father would know that. He'd know that there wouldn't be one chance in ten thousand of catching him outside the house, and he certainly wouldn't dare go inside. So why . . . ?"

"I don't know," I said. "I mean, maybe he wasn't being too logical. He was . . ."

"I understand. He wanted revenge, and he wasn't much concerned with the cost. And since you planned on leaving, he had to commit the murder last night if he was going to do it at all. . . . Yes, it could have been that way. He wasn't sure he'd find Mr. Ontime outside the house, but the possibility existed, and, unfortunately, materialized. But"—he shook his head again—"it still doesn't quite work out. I can't quite get over the idea that the murder was the result of a quarrel; that it wasn't premeditated."

"But you just said . . ."

"Without regard to the murder instrument, Tom. That's difficult to account for on any basis. Matthew Ontime was a strong, vigorous man. With so many other truly deadly weapons available, why should your father choose a pocketknife to kill him?"

"Because he had to. He had to use my knife in order to pin the murder on me."

"But the odds were all against his being able to kill with it. The chances were that Matthew Ontime would take it away from him before he got in one blow."

"Pa would take that chance," I said. "If he was mad enough, he just wouldn't care what happened."

"Yes, but ..."

Miss Trumbull cleared her throat. "Our job, as I see it, is simply to establish Thomas' innocence. What's so difficult about it? This— this Mary woman has it in for Thomas, and she's completely dominated by his father. She's let him do her talking for her, and the sheriff hasn't had any better sense than to let him. What needs to be done, is to get her off by herself. Throw a good scare into her. I'll bet she'd change her story fast. She'd forget all about this neat little alibi which places Carver innocently in bed at the time of the murder."

"But that still wouldn't prove that he did it."

"We don't need to prove it. It would prove that he and she were both liars, that their testimony as to Thomas' probable whereabouts was inspired by pure malice. That's all we need to prove. The rest is up to the sheriff."

Mr. Redbird hesitated. "Well," he admitted, "it would certainly *help* to break down Mary's story."

"Just help?" I said. "I can't see why it wouldn't do the whole job. I mean, it's like Miss Trumbull says. The rest is up to the sheriff."

He looked down at the carpet, not saying anything. I waited and then it came to me: what he was thinking and didn't want to say.

"I see," I said. "It was my knife and I can't prove that I lost it and—and I've acted pretty hot-headed. I slipped up to the plantation before after they'd all gone to bed. It looks like I'd be a lot more likely to go about a killing without figuring out the details than Pa would."

"That's about the size of it," he said soberly. "Now, if your father and Mary would swear that you weren't—"

"It wouldn't do any good, now."

"Well, it certainly wouldn't be as effective as if they'd done it in the first place. But . . ."

"Just a moment." Miss Trumbull banged her coffee cup into her saucer. "You two keep going off on tangents. Let's get back to Thomas' father. Naturally, he's not going to do anything to assist the son he tried to incriminate, and there's no use discussing it. What we need to do is to prove that his alibi is false. When we do that we'll prove a great deal more than the fact of his lying. Don't you see? Why else, unless he committed the murder, would he need an alibi?"

A big smile began spreading over Mr. Redbird's face. He slapped his knee suddenly. "Why, of course," he said, laughing. "That's my devious Indian mind for you; I can't see the pit for the snakes. In all likelihood, Tom's father told Mary he'd committed the murder. He'd want her to be prepared. Of course, her testimony would only be hearsay, and we're still faced with the matter of the . . ."

"We are not!" said Miss Trumbull firmly. "The sheriff is."

"I stand corrected. I'd feel a lot better if—well, I stand corrected," he smiled.

"Good," said Miss Trumbull. "Now, I—more coffee? Well, I guess I won't either, then—now, I suppose it's too late tonight to do anything, and we'll hardly have time before school tomorrow morning. Do you suppose we could get away early in the afternoon, around two, say?"

"We'll do it, whether we can or not. I'll talk to Blunden—explain that we have a strong personal interest in the matter and that we want Mary given a thorough grilling."

"And we'll go right along with him to see that he gives it to her," said Miss Trumbull.

"Right." He stood up, brushing the tobacco crumbs from his trousers. "Tom's going to stay here, is he?"

"Why, yes, naturally." Miss Trumbull frowned. "Where else would he stay?"

"Well, I was just thinking. If it became known that he was here, it . . ."

"I don't need to stay," I said. "I'm feeling fine now. I can . . ."

"No, no," Mr. Redbird said quickly. "I didn't mean that you should hide out. My thought was that you might be, uh, doing yourself a disfavor by remaining a fugitive."

"But—but I have to," I said. "What else can I do?"

"Nothing," said Miss Trumbull. "You'll stay right here until this is all cleared up. I'll keep the shades drawn, and you won't answer the door or telephone and everything will be perfectly all right."

Mr. Redbird hesitated; then his smile came back, and he put out his hand. "Of course, it will be all right," he said. "After all, it's only a matter of a day. Less than a day, actually."

We shook hands and said goodnight. Miss Trumbull walked downstairs with him to the door, and they stood talking for several minutes before he left. I couldn't hear what they were saying, but it sounded like they might be having a kind of argument. Finally the door closed and Miss Trumbull came back upstairs.

She started stacking the trays and dishes together, then paused and looked at me. "Now what's the matter?" she said.

"Are you sure you want me to stay here?"

"If I didn't, I'd tell you so," she said; and I knew she would, too. And I smiled.

"Anything else?" she said. "Out with it. May as well say it as think it."

"I don't really think it," I said. "I was just wondering if . . ."

"Well, stop wondering. Mr. Redbird's concern is all for you—not for himself or me. He's your good friend, Thomas. Remember that, no matter how he acts."

"Yes, ma'am," I said. "I think the world of him, too."

"Good. Keep right on thinking it. Now, go to sleep."

"Yes, ma'am," I said.

And I did.

I didn't wake up until around ten the next morning; and she'd gone, of course, but there was a note for me propped up on the dresser. It read like this:

Do . . .
Eat breakfast in warming oven
Sandwiches (lunch) in refrig.
Rest as much as possible
Make yourself at home

Don't . . .
Worry
Attempt housework

Miss T.

She'd washed and ironed my clothes, and laid them out on the chair. I took a long hot bath, put them on and went down to the kitchen.

There was a platter of ham and eggs and biscuits in the oven, and the coffee pot was half full and still warm. I sat there eating until there wasn't so much as a crumb of biscuit left, and the coffee pot was empty. Then I put the dishes in the sink, and went back upstairs with a book. I took my shoes off, and stretched out on the bed; but the way I was feeling I just couldn't read. I was feeling so good, that is. I was still pretty stiff in the legs but in my mind, the only way that really counts, I'd never felt better in my life.

This time yesterday, I'd been wading up that icy creek on a pair of twisted ankles and I hadn't had a hope in the world. And now, here I was, all nice and clean and warm, and I had hope and something better. When you just hope, you're not sure, and I was sure. I knew everything was going to be all right.

I reckoned that there wasn't a man in Oklahoma that had two finer friends than Miss Trumbull and Mr. Redbird. And I wouldn't let them down either. I'd make 'em proud of me; I'd show 'em I had the stuff in me that they believed I had.

I lay back with my hands locked behind my head, wiggling my toes, grinning and squirming now and then out of pure good feeling. I thought back over the past—the times I'd gotten way out of line—but I wouldn't any more; and I'd do what I could do to swing the others around to the right way of thinking.

Because our thinking, it looked like to me, was at least two-thirds of what was wrong with us.

We were trying to support two civilizations side by side; three, if you counted the Indians. And there wasn't any land ever good enough to do that. And we were always halfsore and suspicious of each other—fighting each other instead of getting at the root of the trouble.

Looking back, I could see that just about all the mess I was in was due to the wrong kind of thinking.

Abe Toolate had tried to get me in trouble. But I could have avoided that trouble if I hadn't prodded him about his race.

Chief Sundown had tried to whip me off the plantation, and naturally I didn't like it. But what had really riled me—the thing that I'd dreaded having known and couldn't stand teasing about—was the fact that *he'd* done it.

And Mr. Ontime. Cantankerous and mean as Pa was, he'd never have talked and argued that way with a white landlord.

And—

But I wasn't going to go along that way any more. I'd get some kind of little job around town so's I could finish high school. I'd go on to college—get some law training, anyway. That was the place to begin, to start changing things: the law. And . . .

And Donna. Well, she'd feel pretty strongly about Pa, naturally, but she wouldn't feel any stronger than I would. And I had a few things to forget myself. So that would be all right; it would all work out in time. And if I could see that I was going someplace—and I would be—it would be all right about her money . . .

I raised my head a little, and looked at the clock on the dresser. It was almost noon, but I wasn't even half-way hungry.

I yawned and lay back down. I pulled the comforter up over me. I sighed, real long and deep and slow, and closed my eyes.

Friends, I thought; the finest a man could have. It takes real trouble for a man to find out who his friends are.

I went to sleep.

I woke up at five-fifteen when the alarm on the dresser clock went off. I guess Miss Trumbull kept it set for that time and forgot to change it when she brought it into my room. It was hard to believe I'd slept that long. I wondered what was keeping Miss Trumbull and Mr. Redbird.

I went into the bathroom and washed and combed my hair. I came back into the bedroom and put my shoes on. I began to get a little worried. I didn't see how anything could go wrong, but—and it wouldn't either! How could it with *them* on my side? I snatched up the book, kind of mad at myself for worrying, doubting, and tried to read.

They'd be here any minute now. Any minute. *I listened to the clock ticking the minutes off.* Any minute and—sure enough.

They came up the stairs together, Miss Trumbull walking in

front; and they seemed to be coming awful slow. But, naturally, it would seem slow to me.

They came in and I started to stand up. And then I let myself down on the bed again.

"Is . . . There's something wrong," I said.

"Bosh!" said Miss Trumbull. But her eyes shied away from mine. "Nonsense! How are you feeling?"

"Fine," I said. "But . . ."

"We've had a little setback, but we'll work it out. Just don't go getting yourself in an uproar. All we need to do is keep our heads— and . . ." She turned quickly and started for the door. "Mr. Redbird will explain to you. Now, you heed what he says, Thomas!"

"Yes, ma'am," I said, "but . . ."

"No buts about it. You just—I'm going down and fix dinner."

She hurried out, bumping into the door jamb as she left. Mr. Redbird sat down and began filling his pipe.

"Tom," he said slowly, "will you do me a favor, something that's very hard to do?"

"What about Mary?" I said. "That's all I want to know. Did she . . ."

"No, that isn't all you want to know. Miss Trumbull and I and the sheriff spent most of the afternoon out there. She and I have gone over all the circumstances of Mr. Ontime's death. We've found out . . ."

"But that doesn't matter!" I said. "All I want to . . . It's like Miss Trumbull said last night. All we have to do is . . ."

"And perhaps you remember my attitude last night." He gestured with the pipe stem. "Now, listen to me, Tom. I want you to understand exactly what you're up—what the situation is."

"But—"

"Will you listen to me, Tom? Will you start doing me that favor right now?"

"But I ..." I swallowed, and broke off. "All right," I said.

He took a long pull at the pipe, then leaned forward, his arms resting on his knees. "So far as can be determined," he said, "Matthew Ontime went to bed at ten-thirty. Just when he got up and went outside again, no one knows. No one heard him or saw him. His rooms are at the rear with their own entrance, so arranged that he could go in and out without disturbing the household. Thus, he may have got up a few minutes after he supposedly retired or it may have been immediately before the murder . . ."

He paused a moment, frowning down at the carpet.

I said, "I still don't see . . ."

"Let me tell you. Or let me ask you a question. You'd been seeing Donna secretly for a long time. You were sweethearts, and obviously you'd talk a lot together. Personal, intimate stuff. Did she tell you— were you familiar with the living arrangements there at the plantation? You knew where her room was, you say, but did she tell you . . . ?"

"I—I'm not sure," I said. "I don't remember that she did, but she might have."

"I see."

"What does she say?"

"Well"—he hesitated—"now, she's understandably overwrought, and she's not absolutely positive, but . . ."

"She's probably right," I said. "Go on. Let's have the rest of it."

"Take it easy, Tom. I'm not telling you all this because I like to."

"I know," I said. "I'm sorry, Mr. Redbird."

"Now, the night of your fracas with Chief Sundown. After he'd interfered, did Mr. Ontime tell you he wanted to talk to you?"

"I guess you know he did," I said.

"And you simply walked off without answering him?"

"Yes," I said, "and I didn't make any appointment to see him later. I didn't go back up there and . . ."

"Tom."

"Well, I didn't," I said.

"I know that. Now, will you let me go on? Good! . . . Mr. Ontime wasn't fully dressed. He was wearing house-slippers, and he had a jacket pulled on over his undershirt. But he did have his trousers on, and his wallet, containing approximately two hundred dollars, was in them. And it was still there, intact, when his body was found. In other words, robbery wasn't the motive for the murder . . ."

"Of course, it wasn't!" I said. "I told—go on."

"He was stabbed from the front. Obviously he was acquainted with the man he had to deal with and he wasn't alarmed by him."

"He knew him, all right," I said, "and he wouldn't have been afraid of him."

"The man killed him, stabbed him to death. Then he lifted his body up over a five-foot fence and dropped it down inside. That's it, Tom. That's the whole story. You need and are entitled to all of it, and I've given it to you. Let's go through it again, point by point:

"One"—he held up a finger—"your father wasn't familiar with the Ontime living arrangements. Two: Mr. Ontime would never have left the house to see him; he'd had his say to your father, and that say was final. Three—and this is the real clincher, Tom—he simply couldn't have lifted Mr. Ontime over that fence. It would have been a physical impossibility for him to do it."

He nodded to me soberly; and I felt the blood moving up into my face. My hands trembled and I shoved them into my pockets.

"He did do it!" I said. "He was the only one that could have. It wasn't a robbery. Mr. Ontime got along fine with everyone else. Pa was the only one that had any reason to kill him. I don't know how he did it. I know it looks like I did, and I don't need anyone to tell me or go out and see how much more they can dig up against . . ."

"Tom! Stop right there!"

"I thought you were going to talk to Mary. Make her tell the truth. That's all you had to do. She'd have broken down fast. Why didn't you just do that instead of . . ."

"Tom. *Tom!*"

"I . . . yes, sir," I said.

"We did talk to Mary. The sheriff took her back and forth through her story a dozen times, and he couldn't shake it. And he would have if she'd been lying. You'll have to face it, Tom. Your father did not kill Matthew Ontime."

"But I—he . . ."

"I know. He and Mary could have removed you from suspicion—largely removed you from it—with a word or two. And they did the opposite instead. But that is no evidence at all that he killed Matthew Ontime, particularly in view of the evidence to the contrary."

"B-but—but there's no one else," I pointed out. "No one but me."

"Yes, there is. There's the man who did the killing."

"But who—No one else had any reason to! If Pa didn't do it, then it has to be me. Everything about it looks like it was me! They'll never look for anyone else. They'll never find . . ."

"They don't need to, Tom. We don't need to. All that has to be done is establish your innocence."

"All?" I laughed kind of wildly. "All?"

"Yes, and we'll do it, too. This case will look entirely different in the hands of a good lawyer. And we'll see that you have a good one."

I stood up. "I appreciate that, Mr. Redbird," I said. "That's mighty fine of both of you, but it wouldn't do any good. The best lawyer in the country can't change facts. I wouldn't stand a chance. All I can do now is . . ."

"No, Tom." He shook his head. "That's the one thing you can't do. That's tying the rope around your own neck. Don't you see? People only *think*, now, but if you run they'll know. They'll conclude that you don't dare face trial."

"And they'll be right," I said. "Gosh, Mr. Redbird, I don't see how . . ."

"Sit down," Tom, he said quietly.

"I don't think I'd better. The quicker I . . ."

"Sit down," he repeated.

"Well, now," I said, sitting down. "Well, now, I sure hope you won't try to stop me, Mr. Redbird. I've trusted you. You and Miss Trumbull are my friends, all I've got in the whole world. But you're not me, Mr. Redbird. You're not the man who's maybe going to the chair. You're . . ."

"You're not either, Tom. You're innocent and we'll prove it. But if we let you run away—then that would be the end of you. They'd catch you in no time at all, and you'd stand convicted before you ever had a trial. Or they'd hunt you down and shoot you trying to escape. I . . ."

"I'll take the chance. At least I'll have a chance."

"No, Tom."

"Mr. Redbird," I said. "I'm asking you to get out of my way."

"No."

We were both standing, now, and I was trying to move around him. He put his hand against my chest and pushed. He kept saying, "No, Tom, no," and I didn't want to do what I could have done. So I just elbowed his hand down and grabbed him by the shoulders. I started to swing him around, and—

Someone was pounding up the front steps, banging on the door; three or four people it sounded like. And I stood listening, still holding on to Mr. Redbird, staring into his eyes.

And I could feel my own eyes getting wider and wider.

The door opened, and Miss Trumbull was saying, "Oh—oh, my goodness! Would you gentlemen mind waiting just a few minutes. I'm afraid . . ."

And another voice, "Well, now, I reckon we've waited a little too long already, Miss Trumbull, and I can't say as I appreciate the way . . ."

I took my hands away from Mr. Redbird's shoulders.

I rubbed them up and down against my shirt.

"I trusted you," I said.

"I'm sorry, Tom. We're only doing what's best for you."

"I trusted you," I said. "You were my friends."

Then they were in the room, and I was holding out my hands, my wrists. I was still staring at him, my eyes getting wider and wider, as they snapped on the handcuffs.

Chapter Fourteen

THEY KEPT THEIR WORD to me, Miss Trumbull and Mr. Redbird did. They got me a lawyer and he was a good one; one of the best criminal lawyers in Oklahoma or anywhere else.

I didn't want them to do it. I wouldn't talk to them when they came to see me. And the judge made it clear to me that I was entitled to counsel of my own choosing. So I'd just about made up my mind to take an attorney appointed by the court. But this lawyer, he was from Oklahoma City and his name was Kossmeyer—"Caustic" Kossmeyer the papers called him when they weren't calling him something worse—this lawyer came to see me, and the first thing I knew . . .

I didn't speak or look up when the jailer let him into my cell. I just sat on my bunk, looking down at the floor, like I'd been doing; and the jailer locked him in and went away. But I couldn't sit that way forever—and it looked like he was prepared to stay that long—so finally I looked up.

And it sounds crazy, the spot I was in, but I burst out laughing. I just couldn't help myself.

He was a little fellow, barely five feet if he was that, and he wouldn't have weighed more than a hundred pounds with his clothes wet. He didn't actually look like me at all, but he was looking like me now; in a way, say, that a cartoon will look like a man. He had his lips pushed way out, and his mouth pulled way down until the corners almost met under his chin. His eyes were rolled down and in, looking at the wisp of hair he'd pulled down over his forehead.

I didn't want to laugh; I was in pure hell and he was poking fun at me. I tried to scowl, and his face shifted a little, and he was scowling. And looking twice as funny as he had before.

And I couldn't hold in any longer. When Kossmeyer wanted you to laugh, you laughed, and he wanted me to. And I did.

He tossed his briefcase into the corner of the bunk and sat down beside me.

"I'm Kossmeyer," he said, as though he was telling me something he didn't really need to: like you might say, I'm the President of the United States. "I'm your attorney. You're my client. Now where can I buy about a thousand feet of calf rope?"

"Calf—?"—I'd stopped laughing. I said, "About your being my attorney, Mr. Koss . . ."

"A thousand feet," he said, "and we're going to need every goddam inch of it. Because we're going to screw 'em, kid. They're going to be screaming calf rope from here to Red River." He tapped me on the shirt front. "Yessir, we'll go through 'em like salts through a widow woman."

I laughed, blushing a little I guess; and he grinned and nodded.

"That's better," he said. "Did you kill that guy, Tom?" And the way he put it, I wouldn't have minded telling him if I had done it.

"No," I said. "I don't care how it looks, I . . ."

"Right the first time," he said. "Wrong the second. Looks are all we do care about. Now, it looks like you killed Ontime, and frankly that side of the picture we can't change much. We can scramble it up, throw in all kinds of doubts, accuse the prosecutor of wanting to stick you because you're a Baptist and he's a . . . Belong to a church? Well, that's all right. I'll dig up some kind of angle. But we can't really change *those* looks much. All we can do is make 'em harder to see, change the looks of something that can be changed. Know what I mean?"

"I guess I don't," I said.

"I understand there's lot of hunting down here. What's the penalty for shooting a possum hound?"

"Huh?" I frowned. "Why no one would do a thing like that. They'd throw you so far into jail you'd never find your way out."

"What about rattlesnakes? Any penalty for shooting them?"

"No, of course not. No one wants rattlesnakes around."
He nodded, and I waited for him to go on. But he seemed to be through. He was waiting, apparently, on me.

"Oh," I said, finally, and I shook my head. "That wouldn't work, Mr. Kossmeyer. It'd be hard to find a finer man than Mr. Ontime and I'd be the first to say so."

"That's the way he *appeared*," he said.

"Anyway, I didn't kill him. So . . ."

"It *appears* that you did. We deny it, naturally; we throw in the old doubts by the armload. But we can't and won't win that way. For all practical purposes"—he tapped me on the chest again—"we're not going to let 'em try you. We're going to try him and her."

"Donna? No," I said. "Not if you mean what I think you do."

"Let me tell you something, kid. There's just one thing that people never get over. Being dead. Anything else can be patched up, and when I say that I'm talking from experience. I defended a madam one time; mayhem and attempted murder. She'd put a bullet through her gentleman friend's head, and damned near sawed him in half with a razor. Now, he was a hell of a nice guy; honest, easy-going, had his own business. In fact, the whole trouble had started when he threatened to drop her if she didn't get out of her racket. I said to hell with the facts, to hell with the way things look. He's an okay guy, I said, and he doesn't really want this beautiful woman hung in the smoke-house for twenty years. He's suffered for it and he's entitled to it, and I'm going to keep her out where he can get at it when he cools off. So I put him on trial. I smeared him like dog crap on a dance floor. I hit him so hard his shirt ran up and down his back like a windowshade.

And the jury wanted to give my client a medal. And about three months later she and this guy got married. . . . That's a true story, Tom. Sometime when you're in Oklahoma City I'll introduce you to them. They're good friends of mine, and one of the happiest couples I know of."

"Well," I said, after I stopped laughing. "I see what you mean. But it wasn't like that with—this isn't the same."

"That's right. This is a capital case."

"I—I just couldn't do it," I said.

"Am I crazy? If you took a step toward the stand I'd murder you myself. You're not going to say anything. All I want you to do is look hurt and handsome, like you wouldn't say crap if you had a mouthful."

"But you'd make her look like . . . I guess not, Mr. Kossmeyer. If I've got anything to say about it."

He shrugged. "All right, Tom."

"What does Miss—what do they think about it?"

"I don't see that they have a think coming. I got a thousand-dollar retainer to come down here and look into the case. All right, I've looked. The thousand's spent. Now, I start all over again."

"Well," I said, "as long as they're putting up the money. . ."

"And you're putting up your life. It's like I said, Tom, they haven't got a think coming. It's your life. Through no fault of your own, and without your consent, you've been forced to trust it to a thing called Justice. And that gal isn't blind, Tom. She's a cross-eyed drunk with d.t.s and a hearing aid, and she doesn't know Shinola unless you shove it under her nose. Did you ever see a man electrocuted?"

"No," I said.

"I have; I've seen any number of executions. Every time I've felt myself getting holy, thinking more about Blackstone than I did people, I've gone to an execution. I've seen 'em die in the gas chamber—

sitting on that little stool with their lips clenched, their nostrils pinched together, fighting to hold their breath until they just couldn't do it any longer. I've ..."

"Don't," I said.

"And the hangings, where their heads come off. Or their necks stretch way out, three or four feet, until they're not much bigger around than one of those bars. But the chair, Tom, that's in a class by itself. I've got a theory about it, and I've talked to some pretty smart people who think I may be right. I don't think the juice really kills 'em. I think it's such a terrific overload for what it has to pass through that it never reaches the brain, all the brain. They still know what's going on after they're taken down to the basement, and their guts are cut out and . . ."

"For God's sake!" I started to jump up but he pulled me back down. "You don't have to . . . !"

". . . and they're tossed into the brine tank. They still know when they're nailed into a pine box and dropped down into a hole in the ground. They go on knowing, thinking, for days, thinking about green grass and sunlight and cool air, and the soft flesh of women and the laughter of little children. And I don't know how they manage it, but—but some of those coffins have been opened up and it seems that they try to get out. It doesn't do any good, of course, but they try to climb back up there with their gutted bellies and their melted eyes, and . . ."

I was sitting with my head bent forward in my hands. Shaking. Sick at my stomach.

He grabbed me by the shoulder, jerked me around facing him.

"All right," he snapped. "That's it. What's a little smearing compared to that? Think about that, and tell me what difference it makes if she used herself for what she was made for."

"I've got to think," I said. "You're probably right, but I'll have to think about it, Mr. Kossmeyer."

"Forget about the goddam money. And don't think I'm handing you charity when I say that. I'm going to wait about a year and then I'm going to send my bill up to that big plantation house, and you'll be right there to pay it."

I didn't say anything. I just couldn't make up my mind. I knew he made sense and I didn't seem to make much—at least, I couldn't put it into words—but I still couldn't say yes like he wanted me to.

"I didn't kill him," I said. "Why can't we work on that, find out who did it?"

"How?"

"Well, I don't know. But . . ."

"Neither do I. And I'm not going to try, Tom. I don't want anything else dug up. There's too much already."

"But . . . Oh," I said.

He nodded slowly. "You say you're innocent. I say you are. And then we just forget about it, because what you and I say doesn't matter. It's what the jury says that matters—what you can make 'em say—and I've showed you the only way to make 'em say the right thing. If they say you're guilty, you are. If they say you're innocent, you are."

"But I *am*," I said. "Don't you . . ."

"Didn't I say so? Tell the turnkey. Maybe he'll let you go."

"I'll have to think about it," I said.

"Maybe there is another way," he said. "I'll plead you insane. It should be easy to prove."

"I can't tell you now," I said. "I just can't and that's all there is to it."

He picked up his briefcase and stood looking at me for a moment.

Then he nodded suddenly as though he'd asked himself a question and answered it.

"All right," he said. "That'll have to do, I guess. I was just about to take a case back in the city, but I think I can hold off my decision a few hours. Of course, it would be much better if . . . But I'll certainly try."

He shouted for the turnkey. He waited, frowning thoughtfully, shaking his head now and then. And I grinned to myself, letting him go right ahead with his little act. I was beginning to understand him, I thought. I could see right through him.

I'd forgotten already, because he wanted me to forget, that you didn't see any farther through Kossmeyer than he wanted you to see.

The turnkey came. Kossmeyer sighed and started for the door.

"Don't worry, Tom. I'm pretty sure I'll be able to make it."

"All right," I said.

"Hell, I'll make it somehow. I'm sure I can. See you in the morning, huh? Bright and early."

"Bright and early," I said.

Chapter Fifteen

I WOKE UP AT daylight; and of course that gave me quite a little while to wait, even if he was early. But that was all right. I'd started thinking things through, and I wanted to have them all clear in my mind before he came.

He'd got me all confused the day before, scared one minute and laughing the next. I hadn't been able to get the real point of things across to him. It wouldn't be enough for him just to get me off. If everyone still thought that I did it—well, where would I be then? How would Donna feel if she went on thinking I killed her father?

Of course, I didn't want to die—it wasn't right for me to go to the chair, no matter what. But if I could just make him understand that I *wasn't* guilty—make him care whether I wasn't—then maybe we could dig up the real murderer. He had to be a local man. He must have left some kind of clues. If they'd really look for him with their minds open, they were almost bound to get a lead on him. I couldn't do anything, but Kossmeyer could. He'd have to, if I could make him understand, because what good would it do if everyone still thought I—

I'd be alive, but—

I'd be alive.

I ate a pretty good breakfast, everything considered. I stood up on my bunk and peeked out the window, and I figured it must be getting on toward nine o'clock. He said he'd be there bright and early. I started walking. I walked back and forth from the wall to the door, less than three good paces.

The turnkey went by the door.

I called out to him and asked him the time; and then he went on past a few steps, like he wasn't going to tell me. He stopped, though, and took out his watch. He dropped it back in his pocket again.

"Ten-thirty."

"Ten-thirty!" I said. "Are you sure?"

He kept on going, not answering me.

I walked some more.

I stood up on my bunk and looked out.

I sat down on the bunk. I lay down. I counted to five hundred by tens, then by fives, then by ones. And still he hadn't come. It was way after eleven. I started pacing again.

He *would* come, of course. He was just playing with me now. He was waiting until I was softened up, ready to say or do anything he wanted, and then he'd show up.

I looked out the window. He'd be here any minute now. He'd said he'd be here early, so—

I stopped. He hadn't actually said so. He hadn't promised. He said he'd try, that he was almost sure he could make it. He—But that was part of the trick. He'd known I'd remember that and start wondering if—

But he *was* a busy man. There were probably plenty of people trying to hire him, people who didn't want a thing but not to die. People with money. And he knew he couldn't ever get any money out of me. He'd get plenty of publicity, of course, and I reckoned no lawyer ever'd had so much he couldn't use more. But . . . but he didn't need to fool around with a guy like me. I couldn't mean a thing to him, really, when you got right down to it.

They didn't serve lunch at the jail, just bread and black coffee. But I couldn't even eat that much. It was all I could do to keep from kicking it over, and slamming it against the walls.

He had another case . . .

He'd said early . . .

He hadn't promised . . .

The sweat ran down my face, and I kept mopping it with my sleeve. But it was sweaty, too. I was all-over sweat, and I had to keep catching myself to stop from mumbling, and—

And I knew that was just what he wanted. I knew he'd planned it that way. But I couldn't be sure. I didn't know. I didn't know. I . . .

And finally I did know. I knew he hadn't been kidding. I knew he wasn't coming. *I knew it.* And I wondered how I could have been so doggone crazy as to hold out against him, and I'd have given anything if . . .

And I looked up, and there he was. Standing at the bars looking in.

"Wait a minute!" He jerked his head at the turnkey. "I'm not sure I'm going in . . . How about it, Tom? What's the answer?"

"We-well," I said, "Can't you . . . ?"

"No."

"But . . ." But I didn't want to die. I didn't want to die. "Come in," I said. "Please come in."

The turnkey locked him in and went away. He tossed his brief-case onto the bunk and looked down at me.

"Uh-huh," he nodded, "but that's a head up there, Tom. That thing you got"—he flicked his fingers across my forehead—"that's a pumpkin. So which one of us do you suppose had better do the thinking?"

"You," I said.

"I didn't stall you simply to swing you around. I wanted to show you what can happen if you try to do your own thinking."

"I got it," I said. "I got the idea, all right."

"Hang onto it. You'll probably never have another one."

I nodded. I'd have nodded or yessed him on anything he said. He sat down beside me, like he had the day before, and slapped me on the knee.

"Good boy. Now, let's get started. Take it right from the begin-ning. How long have you known the gal?"

"Well," I said, "she grew up there on the plantation, and we've . . ."

"I said *known*. In the legal sense. When did you start getting into her pants?"

My face went kind of stiff. I tried to smile, but I couldn't.

"It was over a year ago," I said. "She was pulled up by the side of the road with a flat tire, and I offered to help . . ."

"Naturally, naturally. Poor boy. Big car. Beautiful girl. How could you resist, you in all your innate innocence and courtesy."

"Well it—as a matter of fact, I wasn't real courteous. I was pretty offhand . . ."

"Bashful," he nodded. "Inexperienced. Fighting against the peril you could only sense."

"Look," I said. "It just *wasn't* that way, Mr. Kossmeyer. I know it probably seems funny, it happening the first time we ever really met. But it wasn't. She'd never—she was a virgin, and . . ."

"Did I say no?" He spread his hands. "Sure she was a virgin. And she'd had about all of it she could take. She could have got married, sure, but that would have been too much trouble. And she wouldn't risk her social position with one of her own standing. So she picked on you. Someone who wouldn't dare say anything, and wouldn't be believed if he did."

"But . . ."

"I'm telling you. How often did you see her after that?"

"Well, pretty often. Maybe two or three times a week. But there was more to it than that, Mr. Kossmeyer! We enjoyed being together. We were in love, and . . ."

"That always makes it better," he said. "Where did you meet her?"

"Near the school. She used to park in a place back under the willows, a little off the road."

"Go on. Keep right on talking, Tom . . ."

And I went on. I kept on talking. That day. The next one. More than a week, in all. And he nodded and listened. He listened and kept twisting things around.

"After school," he'd say. "At noon. Sometimes even in the morning. Just wouldn't leave you alone."

And:

"Well, she did tell you where her room was, didn't she? *Didn't* she? And you were up there at her house, weren't you? *Weren't* you?"

And:

"That's a pumpkin, boy. There isn't a goddam thing in it but goo, and it's running out your mouth . . . Sure, you wanted it, but you didn't take it. You wouldn't have dared to take a straight look at this beautiful rich girl, who thought only of her own selfish pleasures. She was beating you with it, kid, that's what happened. She swung at you until you were in mortal fear for yourself, and you climbed her in self-defense."

And, finally:

"Of course she is, Tom. Don't you suppose I know that? She's a lovely, sweet, darling girl, and that's why we can't let her make a serious mistake. And if the game gets rough, well, we don't make the rules."

I was in the courtroom every day, right from the time they started picking the jury. And I'd been dreading that and every other part of the trial, but now I got so I kind of looked forward to it. I don't mean I liked it, exactly. It made me wince a little sometimes to think that this was the law—to know the thinking that was going on behind the things he did. It made me shiver to think what would happen—and probably did happen every day, somewhere—if a man like that was against you.

He'd help some guy down from the jury box, and bow and smile to him and almost shine his shoes. Then he'd sit down at the table with me and pretend to riffle through some papers, and tell me the way of his actions:

"A goddam deacon—a Baptist deacon! Don't they have any Unitarians in this burg? That was one of those eye-for-an-eye boys. He'd have pulled the switch on you himself if he had a chance."

And another time, after he'd accepted two jurors who looked mighty sorry to me:

"Barbers. Barbers and painters and paper-hangers. If you could get enough of 'em, you wouldn't need a lawyer. Carpenters—huh-uh. Their minds seem to move in a straight line. But barbers and painters and paper-hangers! I'd almost as soon have 'em as bartenders."

The county attorney was always watching me, and it seemed to me that he must have just one thing on his mind. And, worried, I mentioned it to Kossmeyer. He grinned, then he looked thoughtful.

"He might at that. He might be stupid enough to ask why you don't take the stand. I'll try to crowd him into it. We're going to screw these bastards, anyway, but a mistrial always helps."

The first day of the trial, the morning of the first day, Kossmeyer moved for dismissal on grounds of insufficient evidence. Then he asked that the judge disqualify himself because he was one-sixteenth Cherokee, and he charged the county attorney with personal prejudice; accepting fees from the Ontime estate.

Well, the judge did have a little Indian blood in him, along with maybe a million other Oklahomans. And the county attorney and almost every other county officer did get little service fees from Ontime, the kind they'd get from any landowner. But all this had to be explained to the jurors, and the more you explain some things the worse they sound.

Kossmeyer got a heck of a bawling out from the judge, and he had to apologize to both him and the county attorney. But as he turned away, he hunched his shoulders and raised his eyebrows at the jurors. The judge saw him and bawled him out again. Kossmeyer apologized again.

He said that he knew he appeared to be a humorous, even pitiful, figure, but God in His wisdom has chosen to make him thus and he hoped that the court would bear with him with the resignation which he was forced to bear with himself. He said that he understood this was hard to do for those who had been carefully nurtured and tended until their bodies became strong and handsome, but—

The judge ordered him to sit down, but he looked pretty uncomfortable. He was six feet tall and he weighed two hundred pounds.

"You see, kid?" Kossmeyer told me that night. "We've got 'em dodging already, him and the c.a. No matter how they play it now, they're always a little in the wrong. If they get tough, they're sore. If they don't, they've got a guilty conscience."

"I see," I said. "How soon do you think I'll be free, Mr. Kossmeyer?"

"Free!" he said, startled.

And I was thinking what I was going to do when I did get free—how I was going to face Pa with the axe in my hand.

"Yes," I nodded. "How long do you think the trial will last?"

"Three weeks, perhaps," he said; and he left soon after that.

As it turned out, it was three weeks before the case went to the jury. But, for all practical purposes, the trial ended on Friday of the second week.

Donna was on the stand; she'd been there day after day. And Kossmeyer was leading her back and forth over the same thing, phrasing the same questions in a hundred different ways and making her answer them, until it sounded like she'd never done anything else but . . .

Chapter Sixteen

"I OBJECT! AGAIN I object to this entire line of questioning, and I am amazed that your honor . . ."

The judge's gavel came down with a bang. "The prosecution will refrain from mention of his emotions or the source of their inspiration. However! Due to the seriousness of this charge, Mr. Kossmeyer, I am allowing the defense the greatest latitude possible, but I am inclined to feel that . . ."

"I shall connect everything up, your honor."

"I feel obliged to warn you again that . . ."

"I am quite sensitive to the court's warnings. I might even say I am becoming intimidated by them. I have been warned about my posture, the tone of my voice, the nervous tic acquired in childhood, the . . ."

"Mr. Kossmeyer, you are in contempt of court. You will leave one hundred dollars with the clerk at the close of today's session."

"I shall have to ask the court's forbearance for a few days. As the court knows, my client has no funds and my resources have been seriously strained by . . ."

"You're breaking my heart."

"I am relieved to learn that the court has . . ."

"Yes?"

"May I proceed?"

"You may!"

"Thank you, your honor," said Kossmeyer, and he turned back to Donna.

"Now, let's see. I wonder if I might ask the reporter to—oh, never mind. I seem to recall the topic under discussion. (Laughter.) By the way, that's a very attractive suit you have on."

"Thank you."

"I notice that the skirt is equipped with zippers . . ."

Laughter.

"*I object!*"

"*Mr. Kossmeyer!*"

"Now," said Kossmeyer, "I believe we agreed that during the course of your, uh, active association with the defendant, you were probably intimate with him a hundred times . . ."

"Yes."

"Give or take a few dozen . . ."

"Your honor, I demand that . . . !"

"Sustained. The remark will be stricken."

"Could it have been as many as a hundred and twenty-five times, Miss Ontime?"

"It could have been."

"But no children resulted?"

"No."

"Your honor, all this has already gone into the record, and defense counsel can have no legitimate purpose in . . ."

"Oh, let it go," said Kossmeyer. "You used contraceptives, Miss Ontime, is that correct?"

"Yes."

"*You* did. You supplied the money for them. You purchased them in another town. You did it, not he. Is that right?"

"Well, naturally, he . . ."

"Just answer my question, please."

"Yes."

"With the intent and purpose of preventing human life?"

"I—yes!"

"You don't have a very high regard for human life, do you,

Miss Ontime?"

"Objection! your honor . . ."

"For certain specimens of it, no," said Donna.

"Sustained. Strike it. The witness will wait for the court's ruling, hereafter, before responding to questions."

"How many times did you receive the defendant in your bedroom, Miss Ontime?"

"Never!"

"Are you quite sure of that? After all, you seem to have satisfied your appetite in virtually every other place. Why not in the natural habitat for such activity?"

"Objection!"

"Mr. Kossmeyer. Just when are you going to connect this decidedly peculiar line of questioning to the case at hand?"

"Very soon, your honor."

"I shall depend on that. Witness may answer."

"I'm sure he was never in my bedroom?"

"Why not, since . . ."

"Because. He just wasn't!"

"Oh," said Kossmeyer, slowly. "You were afraid your father would object?"

"Of course he would have objected!"

"I see. You hadn't told him, then, of your affair with the defendant?"

"Naturally I hadn't!"

"You were afraid to tell him?"

"I—yes. No! I just didn't want to tell him!"

"You wanted to keep it secret, right? Not only from him but everyone else?"

"I . . . I suppose so."

"It didn't make any difference to you, did it, if, to conceal your affair, an innocent man—an innocent victim of circumstances . . ."

"Objection!"

"I withdraw the question. Now, let me ask you this, Miss Ontime. Did you ever invite the defendant to visit you in your bedroom?"

"No!"

"Are you very sure of that?"

"Well—I might have asked him. But I was just . . ."

"Did you ever invite him to visit you on the plantation grounds? Under the shrubbery, say?"

"No!"

"You're sure?"

"I'm positive!"

"Thank you," said Kossmeyer. "Now let me see if I have the situation straight. You asked him to come to your bedroom, but he didn't come. But you *didn't* ask him to visit you on the grounds, and he did come? Is that what you expect us to believe, Miss Ontime?"

"I don't care what you believe!"

"I'm sorry you don't care what we believe, Miss Ontime. A man's life is at stake, and most of us—these good jury men—are here at considerable sacrifice. But . . ."

"Counsel will save his orations for the newspapers."

"I take no exception to that, your honor. I find our American press much fairer than some of our other institutions. May I proceed with the defense of my client?"

"You may. You may also see me in my chambers after adjournment."

"Now, Miss Ontime, you were saying that you didn't care what we thought, and I suppose a girl who's had every advantage of our civilization with none of its responsibilities—"

"Mr. Kossmeyer!"

"—wouldn't care. Incidentally, what are your feelings regarding the defendant?"

"I hate him!"

"You do? Now, at the beginning of the trial, as I recall, your attitude was more one of sorrow. You were only interested in seeing justice done and . . ."

"I hate him! I hope he dies! I hate hate HATE . . . !" She was rocking in her chair, eyes clinched, screaming, laughing. "I h-hate h-him! I ha . . ."

And Kossmeyer was shouting, "Sure, you do! Because you've been exposed for the shameless, graceless thing you are! That's why you've lied—because you want him to die! Why don't you tell the truth, hah? Why . . ."

The county attorney was yelling objections. The judge was swinging his gavel, *bang, bang, bang,* calling and gesturing to the bailiffs. But Kossmeyer kept on shouting at her.

He kept right on, even after the bailiffs grabbed him and started dragging him from the courtroom.

"You're not fooling anyone! The jury knows what you are! So why don't you tell the truth that this poor misguided youth is too chivalrous to reveal! This youth who stands on the brink of eternity where you placed him! Tell the jury how he was attacked by your father and forced to de—"

That was as far as he got before they dragged him out.

Donna was carried from the courtroom.

Court was adjourned for the day.

Kossmeyer got a five-hundred-dollar fine, and a thirty-day jail sentence, to be served as soon as he could arrange his affairs. But he said it was worth it when he came to see me that night.

"That wrapped it up, kid," he said. "It may drag on for another week, but it's all over with the jury."

"Well"—I swallowed hard—"that's good."

"She'll get over it, Tom. I know people—I don't know a goddam thing but people—and I say she'll get over it."

I knew she wouldn't get over it, but I didn't say anything. After all, he'd done it for me and I'd helped him do it.

"All it'll take is time," he went on. "And, Tom"—he hesitated— "you'll have that time."

"How do you mean?" I said.

"Don't you see, boy? This was murder, the big rap. And they had you cold. We didn't have a card in our hands. We've won—but we haven't won the fight. Only the first round. There'll be others, and we'll win those, too; we'll trim 'em down to size and pick 'em off on points. But, meanwhile . . . well, you'll have some time."

"But you said . . ."

"I said we'd beat the chair, and we have. And we're goddam lucky to do it."

"I wonder," I said.

Chapter Seventeen

THE JURY WAS OUT three days.

They brought in a verdict of guilty of murder in the second degree, with an urgent recommendation for leniency.

The judge asked me if I had anything to say before sentence was pronounced.

I started to shake my head. Then I said, "I'm not guilty of murder in the second degree or any other kind."

He sentenced me to twenty years at hard labor at the State Reformatory for Men at Sandstone, Oklahoma.

I turned and looked out into the courtroom.

There was some overlapping, but the spectators were divided roughly into three groups—Indians, whites and Negroes. The white and Negro sections were packed, with people crowding into the aisles. The Indian section—well, that would have been packed except for Abe Toolate. Abe had a whole bench to himself.

My eyes swept on over him, and I remember thinking—and not getting much satisfaction out of it—that he looked as miserable as I felt. Then I was looking at the front bench where Miss Trumbull and Mr. Redbird were sitting.

I'd never really looked at them during the trial. I'd kept from looking at them, and I'd never spoken to them.

Now I looked at them and spoke. I said what Mr. Redbird had told me I would.

"Thank you," I said.

I tried to spot Pa, because I had something I wanted to say to him, too. But he must have been standing in the back somewhere, and . . . And two deputy sheriffs were leading me away.

It was all over.

Chapter Eighteen

"SON-OF-A-BITCH!" *Wha-ack!* The guard swung the strap again, and my whole body jerked against the bars. "You gonna straighten out? You gonna get along?"

"Get along with me," I said.

"Ornery"—*wha-ack!*—"bastard!"—*wha-ack!*—"Say it, goddam yuh! You gonna . . ."

"Hell with you," I said. "You can . . ."

Wha-ack, wha-ack, wha-aack, wha . . .

"That's enough!" The doctor grabbed him by the arms and spun him around. "I said it was *enough!* You don't want to kill him, do you?"

"You're goddam right, I do! I"—the guard was panting, mopping the sweat from his face. "You know how he is, doc! He just won't try to . . ."

"Take him down! Unfasten his wrists!"

"But, doc, you know yourself how . . ."

"I know. But get him down. He can't take any more."

The guard jerked the wrist-straps free. I tried to grip the bars, but my hands were numb and I sagged down to the floor on my knees.

"All right, get some help. We've got to get him to the hospital."

"Huh-uh, doc. I mean, no, sir. He goes to the hole, an' that's orders."

"Not now it isn't! He goes to the hospital!"

. . . I went to the hospital. Again. I'd been in Sandstone a little more than four months, and this was my fourth time in the hospital.

A trusty washed and disinfected my back and put a gauze pack over it. Then he went away, and the doctor stood looking down at me; and finally he kicked a stool up to my cot and sat down.

I liked him. Rather, I would have liked him if I'd been letting myself like anyone. He probably wasn't more than ten years older than I was; and I guess he had plenty to learn yet or he wouldn't have been in this kind of job.

"Well," he said grimly, "how much longer do you think you can go on like this?"

I started to shrug, and the bandages drew. I let out a gasp and he nodded, eyes narrowed.

"Not so good, huh? You keep it up, and they'll be carrying you out of here in pieces."

"I feel all right," I said.

"They'll do it, Carver. They're itching to do it, and it won't cost them a cent."

"They won't do it," I said. *Because I knew I was going to go back. I was going to stand there in the doorway with the axe in my hands.* "I don't give a damn if they do it."

He frowned, puzzledly, leaning forward on the stool. "I know I'm wasting my time, but—I just don't get it. What do you want? What do you expect to gain?"

"I haven't asked for anything," I said, "from you or anyone else."

"But why—what are you trying to prove? This isn't a good stir. There aren't any good ones. Now, there was quite a bit of sympathy for you when you first came here. You weren't a criminal in the true sense of the term. You were just a country boy who'd got himself in a jam with a rich girl, and had to kill her . . ."

I laughed and shook my head. "Never mind me, doc. Go right ahead."

"Everyone was prepared to go easy on you. You could have used your time here to improve yourself. Built yourself up, and made plans for the day when you would leave . . ."

"I've got ..." I broke off the sentence.

"What?"

"Nothing," I said.

"Well . . ." He hesitated. "That's the way it was. This was a great shock to you, a man your age. It seems like the end of the world to you. But, Carver, the fact that you got a twenty-year sentence doesn't mean you have to serve it. You've got a good lawyer pulling for you. Behave yourself, and even if he can't swing a new trial he can get you a reduction of sentence. Why you'd be out of here in . . . well, in no time at all!"

"No time," I said. "I reckon you mean about ten or twelve years, don't you?"

"Well. You can't really expect to . . ."

"I don't expect anything," I said. "I don't want anything. Just leave me alone, doc. Just mind your own business and let me mind mine. That's all the favor I ask."

"You've got it!" He started to stand up. "Do you want a shot? That back's going to give you plenty of trouble tonight."

"Give it to me," I said. "Don't give it to me. Suit yourself."

His eyes flashed and I thought for a second he was going to slam me one. Instead, though, he sagged back down on the stool, staring at me.

"I'm sorry," I said. "But it's like you said, doc. You're wasting your time. No one can do anything for me."

"But . . . why? Why, Carver?"

I hesitated. I didn't see how I could explain it to him when I couldn't really explain it to myself, but he was a good guy so I tried to tell him.

"It's—well, it's kind of like this, doc. Like a story I read one time about a man. He got to where he couldn't see, not really see, you know. He had eyes, but somehow they didn't tell his mind anything. And his ears were the same way. And his mouth. Somehow he couldn't find any words to come out of it; and he couldn't taste anything. Not really taste it. And all over his body, doc, he was kind of numb. He couldn't feel anything. And he knew there was something wrong—he knew what was wrong. But there wasn't a thing he could do about it, him or anyone else. Not a thing, and it was a waste of time to try. Because he was dead."

He waited, as if he thought I might be going to say something else. Then he sighed and stood up.

"Well," he smiled a little. "At least you've talked. That's a start."

"No," I said, "that's the end. There isn't any more."

"We'll see. We'll see about that."

I shook my head. "You wanted to know something. I've tried to tell you. But don't bother me again or I'll tell you something you won't like."

He saw that I meant it.

He gave me a hypodermic and walked away, and he didn't look back. And I was sorry, kind of, but I couldn't help it. I couldn't use any favors. I'd had enough of 'em—things being done to help me, for my own good.

I knew I was going to get out, and I wasn't going to have any help doing it. I'd had help, from Pa, from Mary, from Miss Trumbull and Mr. Redbird, from Kossmeyer . . .

I'd had all the help I was going to take from anyone.

I'd had several letters from Miss Trumbull and Mr. Redbird: Be of good faith. Hold your head high. Things may seem very dark now, but they can change overnight . . .

I'd had a couple of letters from Kossmeyer: "It's taking a little time, kid, but we'll pull it off. Just keep that pumpkin screwed on your neck . . ."

I didn't answer 'em. I'd thought about it, the first letters I got. But then, after a little, it just didn't seem worth doing. It didn't matter, like everything else.

I'd heard from Donna, too—she'd sent me something in an envelope, rather. Because it wasn't a real letter. When I saw what it was, I almost changed my mind about writing to Kossmeyer. I didn't see how he could have done this to me, on top of everything else.

But writing him wouldn't have done any good. And it was beginning to sink in on me that he couldn't make things any worse than they already were. When you're at the end of something, you can't go any further. So I hadn't written.

But I was hoping he'd show up.

He'd said he'd come out to see me, as soon as he had some news. And when he did, I'd have some news for him.

. . . I had about the kind of night I'd expected to have. Worse than any I'd gone through during any of my other times in the hospital. It was daylight before I could go to sleep, and I didn't sleep soundly then. I waked up when I heard the doctor coming.

He took my temperature and glanced at the trusty. "He been getting along all right?"

"Didn't say nothin', didn't ask for nothin'," the trusty shrugged. "You know *him*, doc."

"Yes"—the doctor turned back to me. "How are you feeling?"

"All right."

"Pretty stiff? Want a shot?"

"Suit yourself," I said.

He handed his bag to the trusty and walked away.

He didn't stop by my cot again until four days later. He had me stand up and strip then, while he examined me.

"It's going to be hot out there today"—he was going over my neck, pulling and pushing on the skin with his fingers. "There isn't a breath of air stirring, not a breath, Carver. That quarry dust will be hot as a furnace and just about as thick."

I didn't say anything. I wasn't asking him to do my job, and I wasn't going to do his.

"Those welts are . . . they could *stand* a lot of heeding, Carver. You might be pretty weak yet." He turned me back around. "Or don't you think so?"

"I don't know," I said.

"What would you like to have me say?" There was a little tight-lipped grin on his face. "You tell me, Carver. Ask me. Ask me to say that you can't take the quarry for another week."

"I'm not asking for anything," I said. "I'd just as soon go now."

He hesitated, and his grin went away. But he was awfully young himself, and I'd crowded him hard; and he'd gone too far to back down.

"I'm not sure I heard you, Carver. What . . . ?"

"I'd just as soon go now," I said.

So I went.

A guard marched me down through the corridors and across the yard and out through the gates. I walked five paces in front of him with my hands clasped behind my back, but that—nothing like that was necessary. Not, that is, to keep a man from escaping. Sometimes, quite a few times, a con had stooped down, grabbed up a chunk of sandstone and thrown it—all in one motion. They'd knocked the guards out and killed them with their own guns.

But none of them had ever escaped. The tower guards had telescopic sights on their rifles, and they could pick a man off two miles away if they had to. But they never had to. No one ever got that far.

It was May, and hot like the doctor had said it would be. The heat hit you twice, striking down against your head and neck, glancing up off the rock and getting you in the eyes and face.

I was glad when we got to the quarry. I was getting a little dizzy, and I knew I'd better not. I knew I'd better not fall or stop walking or say anything. The doctor had said I was all right, and that was that.

Usually, when there was a wind, the guards stood way back from the pit. You could look out of some of the cell windows, and see them strung out in a big circle, lounging a couple of hundred yards apart, with that mile-across cloud of dust in the center. Today, though, there wasn't a puff of breeze and they were moved in close so they could call back and forth to each other.

The prison guard left me, and one of the quarry guards took over.

I took off my cap and stuffed it in my pocket. I took off my shirt, folded it and wrapped it around my head. He tossed me a dust mask, and I strapped it over my mouth and nose. It was all stopped up, but it didn't matter. I'd take it off when I got to the bottom. You couldn't get enough air through a mask, and there weren't any guards to make you wear one.

They didn't need guards in the pit. There was no way out except by the ladder. The quarry gangs had so much work to do every day, a certain amount of rock to be hoisted up at the end of the day. And if they didn't have it, they stayed there until they got it.

I edged forward through the dust until I came to the ladder. I wiped my hands against my pants, grabbed the top of the ladder and swung my feet around on the rungs. I went down over the side, and down, down, down.

It was funny about that dust. Up at the top you'd think, well, one thing's sure, it can't be any worse than this. You'd think that every time, because you couldn't see how it could be any worse. And it always was.

It got worse every rung you went down.

After a little ways I could barely see the ladder. Except for the feel, I'd have thought I was gripping dust instead of iron. And I was gripping a lot of dust; dusty mud. My hands were sweating. They slipped against the dusty rungs; you couldn't grip them tight enough to keep from slipping.

I came to a little ledge, a set-back, where the first ladder ended. I hooked my arm through a rung, pulled down the mask, and scrubbed my face against my arm. I started down the next ladder.

I stopped every few rungs or so to wipe my hands against my pants. But they were wet with sweat too, now, and it didn't help much. I whuffed out my nose against my shoulder, but in a moment it was stopped and stinging again. I tried to dig out my eyes with my fists, and it wasn't any good, of course. It was just piling dirt on dirt.

I went down and down, and I thought—I remember thinking—*Now, this doesn't make any sense. A man's got to see, he's got to breathe, he's got to be able to get a grip* . . . And it seemed like a pretty unusual thought.

I stopped and whuffed my nose out good and dug out my eyes, and it helped a lot. And my hands didn't slip any more. Because . . .

Now, this is more like it, I thought. Why didn't I think of this . . .

Because I wasn't holding on to anything.

Chapter Nineteen

I WAS IN THE hospital almost ten weeks, and—And I didn't see that doctor again, the young one who'd wanted to know *why*. He left just as soon as they could get another doctor, before I became conscious, and I never saw him again. And I was sorry about that. Because I didn't blame him a bit. I'd have gotten out of temper with a guy like me, myself, if I'd been in his place.

The new doctor was a man up near his sixties, and he didn't care about whys and whats. He didn't care period. You were just a job with him, and the quicker he got through with you the better he liked it.

He was three weeks finding out that I had anything wrong with me besides concussion and two broken collar bones. Finally, when he got around to noticing that I was passing a lot of blood, he opened my chest and took out the splinters of rib. And I guess he did a pretty good job. But there was quite a bit of infection and it was slow in going away.

I coughed a lot. I got down to where I wasn't much more than skin and bones. And around the temples—well, there wasn't much of it but—my hair turned gray.

It was along toward the end of the sixth week, when I'd started getting a little better, that Kossmeyer came to see me.

I went out to the visitors room, and he looked up from the papers he was reading, then looked back down again. Then he looked up the second time, and a half-dozen expressions flickered across his face in the space of a second. And I knew he couldn't decide on which one to use, how he'd better act.

Finally, he decided and he stood up, wagging his head, the corners of his mouth drawn down. He grabbed my hand, shook it, and pulled me down into a chair beside his.

"Jesus, kid, you look like hell. Think you're going to live?"

"I'll live," I said. "What do you want?"

His expression shifted again. He tapped me on the chest. "Not a thing, boy"—I drew back from his hand, but he didn't seem to notice—"Not a thing—but to get you out of here!"

"Yes?" I said.

"I know. It seems like a long time, and you're sore. But this took a hell of a lot of finagling, Tom. I'm strictly a yak guy, you know. I couldn't do the brief on the case, and I wanted it done by exactly the right guys. The right ones, get me? Two attorneys who used to sit on the appeals bench. So—"

"So you've got me a new trial," I said.

"I ain't done nothing else but, Tom!"

"What'll you get me this time?" I said. "Ninety-nine years?"

"So you're sore. Should I say it again?" He spread his hands. "Now, look, kid. Here's how it stands. I got that son-of-a-bitch—Jesus, that's a lousy jail down there!—I got him reversed on umpty-nine different points. And we're going to go right back before him. We'll get that dirty bastard—I tell you I'm still scratching!—if I have to hogtie him and carry him into court on my back. We'll . . ."

"No," I said.

"You think we won't? We'll get him, and—and that county attorney will be a set-up, too. He'll be begging for a deal, and we'll make like he isn't there. We'll go right into trial, toss 'em all into the suds again. Only this time it'll be lye water. She—they'll be screaming for that calf rope, kid, and that judge won't—I'll have that wall-eyed St. Bernard paying me fi—"

"That's not very smart, is it?" I said.

"What?" He slowed down a little. "How do you mean?"

"About her. She sent me your bill. Marked paid."

"Well . . ." He ran through his expression again; decided on the right act. "You don't mean you're sore about *that*?"

He shrugged and widened his eyes, looking kind of bewildered and hurt, like I'd hauled off and hit him on the nose. And I'd have done it, too, I think, if I'd had the strength.

"Tell me something," I said, slowly, "are you crazy?"

"Actually or relatively? You'd better shake up the seeds in that pumpkin, boy. Didn't I tell you I'd be sending my bill to the plantation? Well. So what if you weren't there yet? Can't a gal write her own checks?"

"Never mind," I said. "Just—never mind."

"Good. Now, I was saying. We'll go right into trial; we'll get everything screwed up good. *Then*, we'll talk deal, we'll let the county attorney talk us into one. And here's what it'll be, Tom. You know what it'll be?"

"Nineteen and a half years."

"Manslaughter. That's the only thing we'll plead to. With the time you've served to equal the amount of your sentence." He nodded firmly, watching me. "We'll get it, Tom. He'll fall over his feet to give it to us."

He waited again, and I didn't say anything; and gradually a look came into his eyes that I'd never seen there before.

"Oh, well," he said, "why am I excited? I've already got my money."

And I'd wanted to hit him a minute before, but now I'd have laid anyone out that put a finger on him. He didn't think like I did. I could never think like he did. But I knew now, seeing that look in his eyes, that what he'd done had been every bit as hard on him as it had on me. Harder, perhaps, because he hadn't been fighting for his life but mine. And I knew that there wasn't enough money in the world to have made him do it.

"Mr. Kossmeyer," I said.

"Sure," he said. "Ask anyone. That's all I care about."

"I'm trying to tell you I'm sorry," I said. "I've been so wrapped up in how I felt, sympathizing with myself, I guess, that I haven't seen how other people might feel. That they might not give way to their feelings like I did."

"Hell! Now you're talking like a . . ."

"You couldn't have made any money on this case. You've probably spent a lot of your own. I don't know why I couldn't see how much it must have taken, that you'd have to have that money from—from any place you could get it to keep on fighting for me. And I should have . . ."

"Will you catch this guy?" He was grinning again, grinning and trying to scowl at the same time. "Wait'll I make him sign a mortgage on that plantation!"

"And I should have stopped you," I said. "But I couldn't see how things stood, and I just couldn't care. I'm sorry, Mr. Kossmeyer. There isn't going to be another trial. I'm not pleading guilty to anything."

"You're not"—he shook his head—"you don't mean that, Tom."

"I mean it. Don't you see? I just couldn't do it. It would be bad enough if I were cleared—if they found me innocent. Even then she'd never be sure that. . ."

"She's sure already. You think she'd have laid out all that dough on you if she wasn't sure? After what I put her through?"

"That's not why she did it. You just don't know her, Mr. Kossmeyer."

"You know how she feels," I said. "You heard her."

"In court. And you heard me there, too. And what did it all mean?"

"That's not the same thing. She . . ."

"Now, you listen to me," he said. "Listen good. You roughed her up when you made a break from your pa's place, and she said things she didn't mean. Then I roughed her up, and she said a lot more. I made her say it. So what? It wasn't because of what she thought you'd done, but the way she felt. And I'd lay you twenty to one that she feels pretty damned sorry about it. She's tried to show you she was, and you're too goddamned stupid to see it. You won't meet her even a tenth of the way. We cut up rough, she cut up rough. It was hard on her—but you really got the dirty end of the stick. You're the one who had to stand trial, and serve time. She helped put you here, and she knows you're not guilty, and now she . . ."

"She doesn't know it. No one knows it."

"You lay—she's practically married to you for more than a year and she doesn't know that? She doesn't know what you're like? She thinks you're guilty, but she doesn't throw a special prosecutor in against me? She doesn't fight a new trial? She pays my bill?"

I hesitated. But I knew what she was like, and I knew what he was like. I knew he could talk a cat into barking if he took the notion.

"Well," he said, "how about it, you stupid jerk?"

"I'm sorry," I said. "I'm sure sorry, Mr. Kossmeyer, after all the work you've done. But . . ."

"But what? What the hell's there to but about? You'd better be thinking about but, kid. Twenty years is a hell of a long time to go without."

"I'm sorry. I just can't do it," I said.

"Tom. My God, boy . . ."

"And I'm not going to be here twenty years," I said. "Maybe that's partly why I can't do what you want. Because I know I'm going to get out, anyway. I'm going to be out before the end of this year."

"Uh-uh"—he jerked his head toward the window. "Out there in the boneyard, you mean. Under it. That's where you'll wind up. They never break out of this place."

"That's not what I mean," I said. "I don't think it'll be that way."

"How, then? If you don't break out or get out on a new trial?"

"I don't know. But I know I will."

I couldn't tell him why I was sure—about the picture I had in my mind of facing Pa with the axe. Because he might have thought it was crazy, but he'd have made it his business to see that nothing of the kind happened.

He told me about the thirty-day jail sentence he'd served; kidding, trying to cheer me up. And it was funny as heck, most of it—all but the part about his last night there. I couldn't get much of a laugh out of that.

"... screwy? Kid, I thought I'd seen some prize goof-balls, but this guy took the cake! They'd picked him up early that evening—Saturday, it was—for being drunk. Put him in the cell next to mine, and he went right to sleep. By sundown, he was as sober as I am now. Get that, Tom; he was dead sober. He knew what he was doing when— Well, I was going to tell you. It looked like about half of the Indians in the county had got hold of a bottle, and the turnkey kept bringing 'em in until there ain't an empty cell left. And then he starts doubling and tripling them up—jamming them into the cells together until they've hardly got standing room. Well, so finally he herds in a fresh batch and stops in front of this cell next to mine, the one the sober Indian's in, and he tells him to clear out. 'Okay, Abe,' he says. 'Hit the street. You're okay, now, and your pals don't want you around.' Abe starts jabbering at the other Indians, and they act like he ain't there. The turnkey tells him to beat it again. He keeps on telling him, and

Abe keeps on jabbering and these Indians keep on playing no-see, no-hear. Finally, the turnkey has to call a couple deputy sheriffs and it takes all three of 'em to toss Abe out of jail. *Out* of it, see? It's the damnedest thing I ever heard of! Can you imagine a guy being so hard up for company that he'd stay in jail to get it?"

"Well ..." I hesitated. "Yes, I can imagine that."

"Yeah? Well, maybe." He shrugged and looked at his watch. "Well, think over that new trial, Tom. You'll see that I'm right."

"I've already thought it over," I said.

"Think some more. Drop me a line at the end of the week. Just write okay on a piece of paper, and shoot it to me. Here. I'll write it for you."

He whipped out a notebook, reached for his fountain pen—and looked at me. Then, he sighed and put the book back into his pocket.

"Well," he said. "I think you're making an awful mistake, but—"

"I can't help it. I can't do the other."

"Yeah. Well . . ."

He stared down at the floor, frowning, scraping a foot against a crack in the tiles. He stood that way a long time, like he was thinking up another argument, and I began to get a little uneasy. I knew that it couldn't be that way, that I couldn't plead guilty. But when I thought about being out there, walking around free, well . . .

When I thought about that I couldn't think much about anything else. Just getting out seemed to be enough—and I knew that it wasn't.

"Y'know"—he looked up at me at last—"I should have my head examined, maybe, but I've just got a hunch. I think you'll do it."

"You don't," I said. "But thanks, anyway."

"Would I lie to you? You're the only guy that has hunches?" He took another quick glance at his watch. "I'll be eating Christmas dinner with you, kid. We'll get her to make a pie out of that goddam pumpkin. The three of us'll eat together. We'll do it, get me?"

"I get you," I said.

"Now, I gotta run. So take it easy and stop acting like a horse's ass, and—and . . ."

And he was gone.

I went back to my cot and lay down.

He'd been so convincing that, for a while, I believed that he meant what he'd said. I could close my eyes and see us eating dinner together, with him joking and cutting up and Donna leaning back and laughing, then turning and smiling at me. I . . .

I could see it for a little while.

Then, it faded away, and somehow it was worse than if I'd never seen it in my mind. There was nothing left but this, and I began to wonder if I was wrong. I began to wonder if there would ever be anything but this. And, gradually, as the days passed, I began to see that there couldn't be anything else.

I'd get out, all right, I was sure of that. And I knew it wouldn't be too long because I was going to see Pa there at the house, and they'd be foreclosing on him in a few months.

I'd be out, but staying out was another matter. Because I wouldn't have that axe in my hands to chop wood.

Everyone would know who'd done it; and even if they didn't know, even if I could figure out some way of getting away with it, I'd know. I couldn't have anything to do with Donna. I wouldn't let myself. So . . .

So it wouldn't matter much whether I was here or not. Less than it mattered now. I wasn't a murderer now, and it looked like I would be. I'd be back. A man has to be someplace, and this would be where I belonged. I'd be here, as long as I lived.

I tried to talk myself into the notion that one part of the picture could come true and the other not. I tried to think of some way I could be out—be there in the doorway of the house—without using the axe. And I couldn't talk myself into it; I couldn't think of any.

The axe was there. I couldn't get rid of it.

And I wasn't going to be chopping any wood in the kitchen.

Once, a couple of weeks after he left, I almost wrote Kossmeyer. I almost told him to go ahead with the trial. Then I thought it over and I saw that that wouldn't really change things at all. No matter how I got out, I'd still be out.

I'd still be there in the doorway with the axe in my hands. Nothing could change that. I knew it as surely as I knew that I was going to leave here before the end of my first year. And I did leave before the end of it.

I'd entered Sandstone in January.

I left in September.

But I'm getting a little ahead of myself.

Chapter Twenty

I WAS IN THE hospital ten weeks, like I've said, and I still didn't have much strength then. I couldn't do anything in the way of real heavy work. But I wasn't actually sick, and you didn't stay in the hospital unless you were, so they worked out a kind of compromise.

They had a few cells on the hospital floor that they'd used for psychopathic cases. But they didn't try to handle people like that any more; just shipped 'em to the insane asylum. So they put me in one of those cells.

The doctor looked in on me now and then, mostly then. I did a little leather-carving by way of work—whenever they thought to furnish me with the leather. All in all, it wasn't too bad. I was a lot better off than most of the prisoners.

The window was way up near the ceiling, and the door was solid, instead of being barred. There was just a little porthole. But there wasn't anything to see out the window but sandstone, and there sure wasn't anything in the hospital I cared about seeing. After I got used to it, it suited me pretty well.

If I hadn't had that axe in my mind, if I'd just been going free and there hadn't been any axe . . .

September came.

And one morning, one forenoon rather—it was a couple of hours after breakfast—there was a rattle at the lock and the door swung open.

It was the warden and the doctor. They looked at me, sort of strained but smiling, like you might look at the town bum who's suddenly struck it rich.

"Well, Carver," the warden said. "I've got some news for you. Good news."

"Have you?" I said.

"The best in the world, and let me say I'm mighty proud and happy for you! Why, I was just telling the doctor here that I always felt you . . ." He hesitated, the eyes in the big, hard red face wavering away from mine. "Well, here. Let you read about it for yourself."

He handed me a newspaper, one of the Oklahoma City dailies. The story was spread across the front page, under a three-picture panel of me, Matthew Ontime and Abe Toolate:

A part-blood Creek Indian, Abe Toolate, confessed last night to the stabbing murder of wealthy plantation owner Matthew Ontime, also of Indian descent, for which another man was tried and convicted. The innocent man, 19-year-old Thomas Carver, has been in Sandstone State Reformatory since January of this year.

According to peace officers of Burdock County, where the sensational crime took place last November, Toolate had been acting peculiarly for several months. Late yesterday afternoon, they said, he came to the sheriff's office and made a detailed confession to the murder. A former school custodian and town ne'er-do-well, he declared that he had killed Mr. Ontime in a moment of panic when the latter surprised him in the attempted theft of a pig from the plantation pens. The murder weapon was a knife which he had stolen from Carver, a high school senior, during his custodial employment.

Attachés of the governor's office revealed that immediate steps were being taken to free Carver. They pointed out that, while the formality of a pardon would take several days, it was within the governor's power to .. .

I looked up. The warden was grinning, his hand thrust out. I laid the newspaper in it.

"All right," I said. "How soon can I leave?"

"Why, uh"—his grin faded. "Why, right away! But I thought we might have a little talk first. I'd like to see you leave here with the right perspective. I, uh, I'm afraid you don't understand that when the courts sentence a man to this institution, we have no, uh, discretion—we can only accord him the treatment which, uh . . ."

"I understand," I said. "Don't worry, warden."

"Worry? Well, now . . ."

"I'm not going to talk," I said. "It wouldn't do any good. This place is like it is for just one reason—because the people don't give a damn. If they did, they'd change it."

His face flamed red. He whirled on the doctor.

"Get him out of here! By God, if I find him here an hour from now, someone's going to—Get him out of here!"

They got me out within an hour. In stiff hard-toed shoes and a baggy black suit with fifty dollars in my pocket. Ten from the state, the rest—I don't know who'd left that on deposit for me. Kossmeyer or Mr. Redbird or Miss Trumbull. I'd never spent any money, because I'd never had any canteen privileges.

I stood outside the high sandstone wall, not moving for a minute or two, somehow afraid to move. Then I began to feel the heat, and I slung my coat over my arm and headed down the road toward town.

It was a five-mile walk, and I'd just missed a bus when I got there. I went into a restaurant, and ordered pie and coffee.

The waitress slammed it down in front of me, staring cold-eyed at my suit. She turned away again, started to pick up the newspaper she'd laid on the back-bar. Then she paused and looked back at me.

The gum in her jaws moved excitedly.

"Why, say—you're that"—she took a quick glance at the paper—"you're that Carver fellow!"

"That's right," I said.

"Gosh, I was just readin' about you! I'll bet you're sure glad to get out, ain't cha?"

I nodded.

"You gonna sue the state?" I betcha they'd have to pay you! You wasn't in very long, o'course, but . . ."

"I guess not," I said. "Like you say, I wasn't in very long."

She drew back a little, looking down at the slopped-over coffee. "Y'know—well, you know how it is. Seems like they all come in here, and they all look alike."

"Yes," I said. "They all look alike."

I was waiting outside when the bus came in. The driver sized me up as I climbed on and jerked his thumb over his shoulder. "In the back, bud."

I sat down on the long back seat. I saw the waitress standing at the restaurant window, tapping on the glass and holding up the newspaper.

The driver swung down to the walk and looked at it. He got back on the bus and came back to where I was.

"Sorry, bu—Mr. Carver. How about comin' up front? Riding gets pretty rough over these wheels."

I shook my head. He started to reach for my elbow.

"Aw, come on; sit up there aside of me. Glad to have you."

"I think I like it better here," I said. And I leaned back and closed my eyes.

A moment later the bus started with a jerk.

I kept my eyes closed most of the way to Chickasha, just opening them now and then, letting them get used to the sunlight gradually. I got off the bus at Chickasha, and bought myself some other shoes and a khaki shirt and pants. I left the prison clothes in the store, and caught another bus. I got into Oklahoma City around five.

I could have got another bus out right away, but I checked the schedules and saw that it would put me into Burdock City around midnight. That was too early. I'd be almost sure to run into someone who knew me if I got in at that time. So I had supper, walked around town a little while, then caught a bus.

It would get me into Burdock City a little after two in the morning. There shouldn't be anyone up and around then; and by the time I walked out to the place, well . . . I wouldn't have long to wait.

The sun was practically set by now, and the evening was cool. I sat next to the bus window, looking out, watching the fields rush by. I'd always liked the fall of the year, better even than the spring. I know it seems like a dead season to some people, with the green things gone or going and the land hard and tired-looking and the birds kind of quiet and soft-singing. But it's never seemed that way to me at all. Me, well, I've never really felt that the green is gone. It's there, right in the fields it came out of, and it'll be right there when spring comes again, all rested and shined up prettier than ever.

The land, now, well I'll tell you how I feel about that. It's done a good job, as good as it was able to, anyway, and it's got a right to look tired. It'd be pretty upsetting if it looked any other way. Yes, and the hardness is all right, too. It's been through something pretty hard, and some of that hardness was bound to rub off. And sometimes a frown sets a lot better with you than a smile. Something that's taken a beating, you don't want to see it laugh. And just because it's stopped laughing doesn't mean it'll never laugh again.

The birds . . . well, I reckon singing never sounds so good, none of the good things seem so good, as when you've been without 'em a while. And good things become bad mighty quick when you have too much of 'em. You start taking them for granted and then they begin getting on your nerves and the first thing you know you're all out of temper, all ready to strike out and snap back at the very things you loved. You're—well, I don't know. Maybe you feel a little guilty, like you're getting more than you're entitled to. And a man may think that's all to the good, but it never is. He's never really content. Probably because, down in his heart, he knows there's no bargains in life. Sooner or later, you pay for everything you get. I—

I like the fall.

I watched the fields rush by, the cotton—they were all through picking in some places—the corn and the cane.

I wondered if Pa had put in a crop on our ten acres, and I figured he probably would have. It would give him a nice little stake to move on with when the mortgage fell due, and . . .

But he wasn't going to need any stake.

He wouldn't be moving on.

It got dark. The bus lights came on, and I couldn't see the fields any more. Just the towns we went through and the lights of the houses sitting back from the road.

I tried to sleep, but I didn't seem to be able to keep my eyes closed. They kept coming open. There wasn't much to see any more, but I went on looking anyway. I kind of felt like there might be something, and I'd miss it if I wasn't looking.

There was a rest stop at Muskogee, and I had some more coffee and a piece of pie. And of course that finished me as far as sleeping was concerned. I'd had more coffee today—real coffee—than I got in a month at Sandstone. I felt like my eyelids were pushed back inside my head.

It was a couple of hours from Muskogee to Burdock City, but when we got there I was more wide awake than ever.

I got off, the only passenger that did. I headed down the side streets until I reached the edge of town and then I took to the fields.

I didn't need to, I guess, because if I hadn't been seen in town, and I hadn't, I sure wasn't likely to run into anyone out here. But I wanted to walk through them. I wanted to feel them under my feet, be close to the growing, rather the grown things.

It was too dark to see anything, but I didn't need to see. You couldn't have lost me out here. I knew my way, where there was a gully or ditch or a fence. I walked down the furrows, brushing against the dew-wet plants, moving from field to field, and I didn't have a bit of trouble.

I began to walk slower.

I was almost there. This was part of our—his workings.

It hadn't been picked yet, the cotton here. I reached down, brushing my hand along the plants, feeling their thickness. I picked myself a couple of bolls and pulled the cotton through my fingers.

It seemed to be a pretty good stand. Should make all of two bales to the acre. If it was picked at the right price and if something didn't happen to the market—

I let the bolls drop from my fingers.

This wasn't ours—his. It was some of the land we'd used to work for Ontime, part of the sharecrop forty.

Our ten acres lay next to this. I pushed down the top wire of the fence, straddled it and stepped over.

I took a few steps forward, quite a few, before I stopped, because I just couldn't believe it was like this. That this was Johnson grass coming almost up to my waist, and that those were sunflowers striking me in the face.

I stopped dead in my tracks, angry, bewildered; not knowing quite what to think.

It just didn't make sense, any way you looked at it. A kid could work ten acres if he had to. And if he, Pa, hadn't wanted to work it, he could have shared it over to someone else. He could have done something with it—he hadn't needed to let it go like this. You just couldn't do like *this*.

You let Johnson grass and sunflowers get a start like they had here, and you'd have to fight 'em for years to come. And they'd spread; you'd make it hard on everyone around you. Maybe the land wasn't yours any more. Maybe you weren't going to get any more out of it. But that wasn't any excuse. You just didn't do this if—

If you were even a tenth of a man.

If you gave a damn about anything.

It was like burning-off on a windy day. It was like, well, standing outside a privy and dirtying your clothes.

I pushed on through the field and came to the fence. I stepped over it and into the yard.

And it was the same way there, the same as the field. He'd—

I stopped thinking about it.

I found the door of the woodshed and went inside.

The whetstone was over the doorsill where it always was, and the axe, like always, was stuck in the chopping block. I jerked it free and sat down on the block, running my hand over the rusted blade. I clamped it between my knees, knocked the dust from the stone and began to whet it.

I'd done it in the picture. I had to do it now.

I moved the stone back and forth across the blade, stopping now and then to test the edge with my thumb. I turned it again and again, whetting it razor sharp, until it had a sweet ring to it when I tapped it with my nails. It was getting daylight now, and the blade glistened like silver.

But there was still time. I still had plenty of time. So I went to work on the head. I rubbed it with the stone, polishing away the grit

175

and rust, and it began to shine like the blade.

I worked on and on, the light going brighter and brighter on the blade. And finally there wasn't any more to do. There wasn't a speck of rust or grit left. It was shiny as a mirror—I could have seen myself in it if I'd wanted to.

There was nothing more to do to it. Only with it.

I took it by the handle and went to the door.

I'd had a pretty good idea of how it would look out there, but seeing it was something else. Weeds, sunflowers, Johnson grass, filling the yard, growing right up to the porch and pushing up under it through the planks. And the house itself, sagging at one end where one of the foundation rocks had crumbled; the house, sunburned of its whitewash, windows dirty, one of them broken and stuffed with rags.

This wasn't the yard I remembered. This wasn't the house. This had never been any part of me.

I waited, listening in the morning stillness.

Faintly, I heard a door creak, and, after a minute or two, the rattle of dishes. They were up—someone was up.

I looked down at the axe, twirled it slowly, watching it glisten in the sun. I pushed through the weeds and the grass and the sunflowers and stepped up on the porch.

I moved over to the door and stopped, looking in at him.

"Hello, Pa," I said.

Chapter Twenty-One

HE WAS SITTING AT the table, eating or just starting to eat, his head bent over a bowl of something dry and powdery. He looked up slowly, raising a spoonful of the stuff at the same time, and some of it moved with his breathing, puffed away from the spoon. And I saw that it was cornmeal—dry, uncooked.

"Pa," I said.

He hesitated. Then he let his head come all the way up until he was looking straight at me. And his eyes and mouth were like holes in the bottom of a dirty nest, in the gray matted stubble of his beard.

"No, sir"—he looked at me, shaking his head—"Can't fool me. You ain't there. You're"—he giggled craftily—"you're there, you prove it. Go'n get her. She's off over to them oil workers' camp. You get her, an' . . . an' you know. Me'n you together, huh?"

And I—

I don't know. I don't know quite how to put it.

Somehow I must have had the idea that everything would stand still; that I'd come back and pick up at the scene I'd left: the two of them here together, unchanged, taking it easy, safe, grunting and struggling through the nights, then lying back gloating, grinning and whispering about the thing they'd done to me. I'd seen them that way in my mind a thousand times, and nothing beyond that. I had to collect for it. For Sandstone. For Donna. For all that he'd taken away from me, while he'd been here, safe, taking it easy while . . .

Safe? Taking it . . .?

I felt lost. Empty.

I should have known, by the way the yard was, the yard and the field and the house, the rot and the decay out there, and the filth and the dirt in here—I should have known that nothing stands still; that there is always change in one way or another—upward or downward. But still the picture had been there, and part of it still was. The one part, the only part, I'd really seen in my mind.

Him sitting there in the kitchen. Me in the doorway. And the sharp, shiny axe in my hands. And I had to use that axe for just one thing, didn't I?

I stepped forward suddenly, swinging the axe back over my shoulder. I brought it down, whistling through the air, and he ducked and toppled backwards, tumbled over in his chair to the floor.

So I did use it to chop wood. I chopped up the top of the table, whacking it into kindling and splinters. And I scooped up an armful, poked and jammed it into the stove and started a fire.

He'd gotten to his feet. He stood humped over, giggling that crafty giggle. I whirled on him, swinging the axe again. I let go of it and it flashed across the room, smacked quivering into the wall of the house.

"There," I panted, "you do that next time. You do it, hear me? Cook. Wash. Chop up the furniture if you have to, but do it!"

"Can't fool me. You ain't really . . ."

"You know I'm here," I said. "You knew I was out there this morning. And all my coming back meant to you was a chance to get something, to keep on taking. Anything. To get a fire built, if nothing more. Anything at all so long as you could *get*—get without putting out. What's the matter with you?" I took a step forward, reaching, but I wasn't going to put my hands on *that*. "You're not sick. What in the name of God is the matter with you?"

But I knew what it was. Because I knew he hadn't changed, after all. He was like he'd always been. Just *more* like he'd always been.

He wouldn't give up, yet. It was his one way left of getting, as he saw it, and it was hard to give up.

"Got to show me. You're Tom, you go an' get her. Bring her back here an' . . ."

"Stop it," I said.

"Gotta have her, an' that'll prove it. You go . . ."

And I laughed, and that stopped him.

"You're not crazy," I said. "You know exactly what you're doing. You know what you've done. You were never thinking sharper in your life, and all you can do with that thinking is this. What do you want it for? What does it get you? Look around you—take a look at yourself and tell me this means something to you. Weeds, filth, the house falling apart, and you sitting here like a—like a toad in a trash pile, sinking deeper and deeper and doing nothing, waiting for someone to . . ."

"Tom. It's been mighty hard here without . . ."

"Here," I said. "It was hard *here!* You tell me it was hard here!"

"But you wanted to go on, didn't you? There wasn't nothin' to go on for, but you . . . went on."

I shook my head. That wasn't the same thing. I couldn't help being in Sandstone; the way I lived there. I hadn't had any choice like he . . .

But couldn't I have helped being there? Couldn't I have helped the things that helped to put me there? Couldn't I have helped the way I lived there, doing nothing for myself but making them keep me alive?

And *did* he have a choice? Had he had one, being what he was?

"All right," I said. "Maybe. Maybe not. I don't care. I don't care what you do or don't do. I didn't come here because I—I—"

Suddenly, I knew why I'd come; and I knew it was ten times worse than the other. Not the clean sharp blow of the axe, to finish everything in a second. But to do what I'd done; chop wood and build a fire and anything else that needed doing. Like this that I was doing now. Trying to find a reason, an excuse, to stay; to watch him die, rot, gradually, little by little while I tried to fight off the rot. Because I'd always done that, and I hadn't really changed any more than he had.

I wished he'd say something. Do something. Anything that would break the link between us, let me turn my back and walk out of here. Let him live as he had to. Let me live as I wanted to. While I still had a choice.

"Tom"—the crafty glitter was back in his eyes—"I know why you came."

"Yes," I said, "I'll bet you do."

"You knew me, didn't you? You knew your ol' Pa'd hide you out. But I'll tell you somethin'—you don't need to hide out. I know who done it, Tom."

"Hide out?" I frowned. "I don't—Oh," I said.

"Uh-huh. I don't get around no more, just don't seem no sense in it somehow. But I hear a thing or two, an' I know who done it . . ."

He knew. He and the whole state of Oklahoma. But he wouldn't see that, he wouldn't think or hear beyond the point of what it meant to him. What he could get out of it.

"You want to know who it was, Tom? You don't want 'em to catch you an' take you back to Sandstone? I reckon you sure don't want that, do you?"

"Who was it?" I said.

"Huh-uh," he shook his head, grinning. "Not so fast. You write out a little note to that Injun girl. Tell her you got to have some money—about a, well, what's it worth to you, anyways? What'll you give me to tell you?"

I sighed, and I felt my shoulders straightening. It was like a thousand pounds had been lifted off my back.

"Thanks," I said. "Thanks a lot, Pa."

"Huh? Where you think you're going? You go out that door, an' I'll . . ."

"I don't know where I'm going," I said. "Or what I'll do."

"I'll sic the law on you! You write that Injun girl or . . ."

"I'll get work as soon as I can. I'll send you a little money when I can. But don't ever try to see me. Don't ever speak to me if you do see me."

I walked out the doorway, and his voice followed me shrieking, *"You'll see! I'll . . ."* But he didn't follow me to the door, and the shrieking stopped in a moment. Nothing was worth any effort. There was nothing that effort would get.

I pushed my way through the weeds, and he was a million miles behind me with every step.

I felt empty but I wasn't hungry; tired but I didn't want to rest.

I plodded on through the weeds toward the road.

My head ached, and my eyes felt tired and hot. I tried to think—figure out what I was going to do. Because I knew the one thing I'd wanted most would be the wrong thing now. Kossmeyer's hunch might be right, but you can't run a life on hunches. She might be willing to start giving again, giving where nothing could be given in return, but you can't run a life on giving. It wouldn't be a good life for either of us.

I could wait. A man does what he has to, and I had to wait. Perhaps we would have Christmas dinner together. If not this Christmas, the next; if not that, the next. The when of it wasn't important, but the how, and what happened afterwards. Afterwards: building something that would last instead of something that the first strong wind would blow away. One thing was certain. When we had that dinner,

I'd have earned it. It might not be anything more than sow-belly and beans, but I'd be doing the giving.

Now, there was work to do, thinking—real thinking, not wishing; so much, so many things, that it was hard to judge where to begin. The past was all mixed up with the future, and I had to sort it out and smooth it out, patch up the back-trail while I got to work on the new one. And I didn't know where to begin. And I had to begin somewhere fast. I had to do something. I felt achy and empty, and kind of scared.

I walked with my head down, seeing nothing but the weeds in front of me, my feet moving one in front of the other. And then they slowed up, all by themselves it seemed like. They stopped by themselves, like they knew a lot better what to do than I did.

I turned and looked back. I walked back.

There was a bird's nest built on the trestle of the well-pull. I reached up and lifted it down, gently so's not to shake the three speckled eggs. Birds couldn't hurt the well water, of course. Not for a man who couldn't taste any more—not really taste—who couldn't

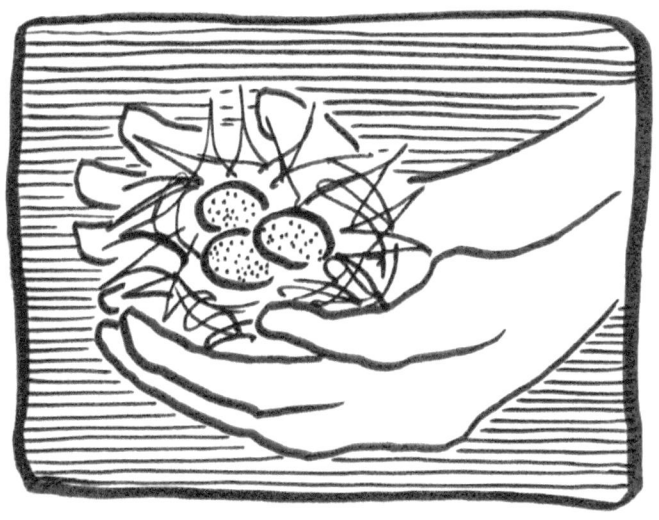

smell or feel or . . . But they might be hurt. They might get too smart and sassy for their feathers, the young'uns, and they wouldn't get another chance at life. If they went down into the pit, they'd stay down.

I walked back toward the road, stepping easy, looking around for a safe fence post or tree crotch I could put the nest in. And somehow my own problems kind of slid away from me. Somehow this was my problem, saving something that might be lost without my help, and there wasn't anything more important.

I reached the road. The grin—I'd started to grin without knowing it—froze on my mouth.

The weeds had hidden the road; so I don't know how long the car had been there; I don't know how long she'd been waiting. And there was nothing in her expression to tell me why she had come or why she had waited. To tell me off, maybe. Or maybe to do the opposite—tell me everything was all right. Probably she didn't know why herself. She'd simply come here because she had to, as I'd had to, and she'd been as mixed up as I was about the next step.

She came forward, slowly, neither smiling nor frowning, her eyes fastened on mine. Waiting, I guess, for me to lead off, say something. And there was nothing I could say—not now, so soon. All I could think of was to turn and run.

She kept on coming, and I began to tremble; in another second I knew I'd be running . . . Save something? Hell, how could a man save something when he couldn't save himself? There was a great silence, and out of it came only one voice, yelling at me to run and keep on running forever. Yelling at me not to do anything, not to try to rebuild. *Because you'll be disappointed, Tom. It just isn't worth the disappointment, and heartbreak. They'll never forget that trial, kid. They'll never let you or her forget it. They'll laugh at you; or, worse, they'll pity you. And you're ignorant, uneducated, and your health isn't good, and—*

What can you do, anyway? What can you rebuild with? Think it over,
Tommy. Think of everything you've got to fight. Keep thinking—that you'll
lose even if you win. Then go and hide. Bury yourself. And stay buried. Run
away from—

Her hands went around mine, steadying them on the nest. And it was odd that they should steady them, for hers were trembling, too, but that's the way it was. Like in algebra, sort of; the two minuses together had made a plus.

The voice stopped yelling at me to run. It saw I wasn't going to, I guess, so it just plumb gave up. It went away and stayed away, leaving us there together. And there was nothing we could say that would've been right—nothing that wouldn't have been as awkward and embarrassed-sounding as we felt. So we didn't say anything, either of us.

We just stood there silently in the November sunlight, kind of stiff and formal-ish; thinking out the next step, getting used to each other gradually. We stood looking down into the nest, wondering, deciding rather, what to do with this new life in our hands. . . .

 THE END

CHALK LINE BOOKS™

Also Available from Chalk Line Books

Night Squad by David Goodis
The Killing by Lionel White
(made into a classic noir film by Stanley Kubrick)

Chalk Line T-shirts

Chalk Line T-shirts, white with black logo, are available in large and x-large sizes for $17.95 each, which includes shipping in the U.S.

Send check or money order to:
Chalk Line Books, 2197 Cowden Ave., Memphis, TN 38104
Allow four weeks for delivery.

JOIN OUR MAILING LIST

We will be glad to place you on our emailing list to receive updates about new Chalk Line releases, products such as our very cool T-shirts, and other things pertinent to our vintage crime fiction. If you join us you will only receive Chalk Line-related information. Your name and email address will not be forwarded to any third party or other emailing list.

Contact us at tom@devault-gravesagency.com and ask to be placed on our Chalk Line email list.

CHALK
LINE
BOOKS™

OTHER EBOOKS YOU MIGHT ENJOY FROM DEVAULT-GRAVES DIGITAL EDITIONS

Three Early Stories by J. D. Salinger

Big Sur by Jack Kerouac

Maggie Cassady by Jack Kerouac

Tristessa by Jack Kerouac

Do You Sleep in the Nude? by Rex Reed

People Are Crazy Here by Rex Reed

Conversations in the Raw by Rex Reed

Valentines & Vitriol by Rex Reed

Weegee: The Autobiography

Black Man in the White House by Frederic Morrow

Crossroads: The Life and Afterlife of Blues Legend Robert Johnson by Tom Graves

www.ingramcontent.com/pod-product-compliance
Lightning Source LLC
Chambersburg PA
CBHW031111020726
47495CB00007B/2146